He was standing behind her.
All six-feet-three-amazing-inches of him.

Sloan drew a quick breath as Aidan turned her to face him. She lifted her chin and his lips captured hers, silencing her in a flash. Her heart leaped in her chest, and she was pretty sure she let out a moan of longing.

He didn't hesitate to tangle his tongue with hers. He tasted of the lemon he drank with his tea. He smelled of sawdust and spicy sandalwood.

She clutched his T-shirt in her fist, grasping to get closer. She wanted to feel his bare, sleek skin against hers, to have that intense gaze focused on her, to feel his muscles harden beneath her...to have him tremble and gasp along with her.

His hands molded her to his body and she felt the need, the hunger and the wild lust they'd been trying to deny. It had been too long, and she wasn't going to miss her chance now that it had come, to satisfy her desires...and his.

Dear Reader,

I'm a Southerner with roots so deep my mother has directly traced me (since I'm the oldest grandchild) back seven generations to my great-several-times-over grandfather, who was one of the first non-Native Americans to live in Reeseville, Alabama.

Along with family histories, telling stories is a Southern tradition, and now that I live in South Carolina, I'm learning new tales to share. Palmer's Island is my fictional combination of two real islands off the coast near Charleston—Isle of Palms and Sullivan's Island. Beautiful and quiet, they represent a beloved living history in this part of the country.

Like any real Southern town, I infused my island with nosy but caring citizens, church ladies who love to bake casseroles and a beauty salon as gossip central. It was also the perfect place for my grieving hero, Aidan Kendrick, to hide and brood in a dark, damaged house behind a wall of tangled foliage. Fortunately for him, however, Sloan Caldwell and her fellow islanders are like the island itself—abundant with sunshine and forgiving of mistakes.

I hope you enjoy my tale of love and redemption—with an old-fashioned mystery mixed in to keep everybody guessing.

Best wishes,

Wendy Etherington

After Dark

WENDY ETHERINGTON

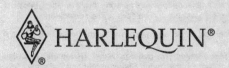

HARLEQUIN®

TORONTO • NEW YORK • LONDON
AMSTERDAM • PARIS • SYDNEY • HAMBURG
STOCKHOLM • ATHENS • TOKYO • MILAN • MADRID
PRAGUE • WARSAW • BUDAPEST • AUCKLAND

Recycling programs
for this product may
not exist in your area.

ISBN-13: 978-0-373-79450-8
ISBN-10:   0-373-79450-9

AFTER DARK

ABOUT THE AUTHOR

Wendy Etherington was born and raised in the deep South—and she has the fried-chicken recipes and NASCAR ticket stubs to prove it. The author of nearly twenty books, she writes full-time from her home in South Carolina, where she lives with her husband and two daughters. She can be reached via www.wendyetherington.com or by regular mail at P.O. Box 3016, Irmo, SC 29063.

Books by Wendy Etherington

HARLEQUIN BLAZE
263—JUST ONE TASTE...
310—A BREATH AWAY
385—WHAT HAPPENED IN VEGAS...

HARLEQUIN NASCAR
HOT PURSUIT
FULL THROTTLE

HQN BOOKS
NO HOLDING BACK, with Liz Allison
RISKING HER HEART, with Liz Allison
A NASCAR CHRISTMAS 3,
   "Have a Beachy Little Christmas"

To my cousin, Mark Durham, a true Southerner
who knows how to tell a good story

1

Sloan Caldwell yanked at the hem of her little black dress, then lifted the worn brass knocker on the big oak door. The resulting tapping noise sounded like a series of gunshots, echoing in the misty, dark night.

Every small town in the South had a crumbling, spooky old mansion on a hill, and hers didn't disappoint—though their hill was more of a dune. To think, they now had a genuinely dark, eccentric and notorious owner to go with it.

It was spine-tingling stuff for Palmer's Island, South Carolina.

As a barrier island just over three miles wide, with five restaurants, one bar, no high-rise hotels, one public park that was beach-accessible and its largest house—the one she was standing on the porch of—not backing up to the beach, the island itself was considered a bit eccentric. But the residents who lived there and the tourists who visited liked it that way.

After several long minutes, the door was flung open. The tall, dim shadow of a broad-shouldered man filled the frame. "What do you—" He stopped, cocking his head. "Who are you?"

Sloan really wished she could see his face, specifically his eyes—though she knew from the TV, newspaper and Internet how gorgeous he was—but the lack of light on the porch or in the foyer left most of the details about him to her memory and imagination.

She swallowed and held out her hand. "I'm Sloan Caldwell, Director of the Palmer's Island Historical Preservation Society."

"*You're* a society matron?" he asked, his disbelieving tone clear.

Like blue hair was a requirement for social awareness. "Miss, actually." She tried a smile and put her hand on her hip. She had nice hips. Men usually noticed. "May I come in?"

He crossed his arms over his chest and leaned against the door frame. "No."

"*No?*"

"I'm busy at the moment. Come back another time." He started to turn away.

She reached into the briefcase hitched on her shoulder and pulled out a file folder, which she handed him. "But *you* contacted *me*. About the renovations to the house?" she added when he remained silent.

Sighing audibly, he reached behind him and flipped a switch, which turned out to belong to a small desk lamp sitting on a sawhorse in the foyer. "My lawyer sent this," he said, staring at the papers in the file, then flicking his gaze to hers. "I didn't contact you."

Silver. His eyes were a cool and piercing silver.

Again, she'd known this both from his recent notoriety courtesy of twenty-four-hour cable news and from the research she'd done on him. But the images hadn't done him justice. The pictures weren't full of annoyance and sensual power. Nor had she been prepared for the breath-stealing impact of having that gaze focused on her. Not to mention the fact that those eyes were surrounded by a lean face, the sculpted jaw shadowed by dark stubble and tons of tousled, wavy black hair.

She shivered. And not in a bad way.

Clearing her throat, she tried to remember she was there on business. "As your lawyer is no doubt aware—even if you aren't—all renovations to Batherton House must be approved by the committee before any work can be done."

"So?"

"Your neighbors heard hammering."

"What neighbors? The property encompasses three acres."

"But past the intimidating, spooky and overgrown bushes and trees, there *are* houses on either side of you. You just can't see them." She smiled in the face of his frustration. "Sound tends to echo out here on the island." She accepted the documents he thrust back into her hand. "I thought I should come out here personally and take a look at your plans."

She could practically see the wheels in his brain spinning, striving desperately to find a way to get rid of her. She found his efforts surprising and interesting. Very few men had the urge to slam the door in her face.

And not just because she was the sheriff's only daughter.

"Do you always come to business meetings at nearly nine at night, dressed like that?" he asked, drawing his eyebrows together.

"I preserve the past, Mr. Kendrick," she said huskily, stepping closer, so that their bodies nearly touched. "But I live very much in the present."

His eyes shone with interest for a split second, then he stepped back.

She walked past him, the faint scent of whiskey brushing by her nose. Drinking alone in a dark old house? Aidan Kendrick certainly lived up to his eccentric reputation.

"I bet you were surprised by the working electrical system," she said, walking across the foyer's wood floors and into the parlor, where she flipped on the switch for the bare bulb hanging from the ceiling. "Old Doc Marcus replaced it about twenty years ago."

"Nothing surprises me, Miss Caldwell." He paused. "At least not until you appeared on my porch."

Smiling, she glanced over her shoulder at him. "I have that effect on some men."

He nearly succeeding in looking amused. "I'll bet."

She wandered around the room, noting the stacks of boxes in one corner, the collection of hand and power tools gathered in another. Wondering about the lack of furniture, she strolled past him. She peeked into the dining room on the opposite side of the foyer, but finding nothing but a creaking and broken chandelier and an impressive collection of cobwebs, she moved into the central hallway and headed toward the back of the house, where she knew the kitchen was located.

Here, at least, there was a battered oak table and a set of chairs that looked reasonably sturdy. There was also evidence that someone actually lived in the house.

A brand-new stainless-steel refrigerator took up one corner. Empty water bottles were strewn across the scarred, yellowing, linoleum countertops. A partial loaf of bread sat next to a plate bearing a half-eaten ham sandwich. A nearly empty bottle of whiskey rested beside a stack of red plastic cups.

The whole place was depressing. It was hard to believe the Atlantic Ocean ebbed and flowed only a few blocks away.

She lowered herself into one of the chairs, set her briefcase beside her, then looked up at him. "It was rude of you not to invite me in. I thought you were from Atlanta."

He frowned. "I am."

"They never taught you Southern hospitality up there?"

"We're a rare breed, I guess," he said, his sarcasm clear.

"For instance, we rarely come uninvited to someone's house, then walk around like we own the place."

She shrugged. "I came to see the house. I didn't see any point in not getting started. Do you ever offer uninvited guests something to drink?"

He crossed his arms over his chest. "I have whiskey and water."

She needed water for her dry mouth. Heavens, the man was so tempting. But she knew he'd smirk at that request. "I'll have whiskey."

"One finger or two?"

"One."

Without comment, he moved to the counter, then poured a splash of the amber liquid into a fresh plastic cup. When he returned to her, he held out the cup.

She didn't quite suppress a wince. "No ice?"

"I haven't hooked up the ice maker yet."

She took the cup, glanced into it, then tossed back the contents in one swallow. Her throat burned, then her chest. But she didn't cough or flinch.

On occasion, she liked the rich, smoky taste of whiskey. However, she preferred it with a serious game of poker. Or a hot fire and a warm guy. Or, even better, a hot guy and a blazing fire.

"Do I pass?" she asked, handing him back the cup.

"Pass what?"

"The test on not being afraid of you."

"I'm not testing you," he said, his annoyance intensifying. "I'm not doing anything with you."

But you could be. She'd never gone after a guy who clearly wanted to see the back of her. In fact, she'd had enough of guys she wanted, but who'd suddenly realized they didn't want her.

Guy, really.

After wallowing in Rejected Land a few months back, she'd decided she liked her guys fun, enthralled and uncomplicated. Which Davis had been. Before he'd decided to run off to Atlanta after some other woman—and a job with the man glaring at her now.

Which brought up a whole new complication. Why had Aidan Kendrick decided to come to Palmer's Island? Did it have anything to do with Davis? How well did the two men know each other?

When her life decided to come full circle, it had apparently chosen to jump on the upside-down roller coaster, rather than the merry-go-round.

"Oh, so you're *not* trying to intimidate me into running back to town and leaving you to your brooding and hammering?"

"Sure I am." His lips curved. "And, yes, you would greatly aid my efforts if you'd saunter back to town."

The effort at humor was intriguing. Appealing. If he could be any more appealing, that is. "I don't saunter."

"Yeah, well, I'm *renovating,* not hammering."

"What about brooding?"

He lifted his shoulders in a careless shrug. "The Irish are entitled."

"I suppose we are."

"We?"

She held out her hand. "Sloan—warrior."

This time he took her hand and shook it. The contact sent a bold shock up her arm. "Aidan—little fire."

He looked pretty cold to her, but there was heat in there somewhere, behind the ice of his eyes. No man could have been through what he had, come through still standing, and not have a flame burning deep inside.

"And I doubt there's much you're afraid of," he added.

"True." She reached for her briefcase, and—again—wished he wasn't so sexy, amazing...*dangerous.* "The blue-steel Glock nine millimeter I carry in my glove compartment doesn't hurt."

SOMEHOW, Aidan found himself sitting opposite her at the beat-up kitchen table. Unwanted desire crawled over his skin, even as part of him craved her brightness.

She was the very last thing he needed.

And the very thing he longed for.

"I'm sorry to call so late," she said briskly, flipping her long blond hair over her shoulder, then digging into her bulging briefcase. "My day job forces me to keep irregular hours when dealing with the historical society business. And since you have no phone, I had to—"

"Day job?"

She glanced up. "I'm a librarian."

"No way." He'd figured pole dancer. Well, her *body* screamed pole dancer. Maybe, subconsciously he was *hoping* for a pole dancer. He let his gaze drift over her buxom figure—all that he could see above the table. Beneath, he knew there were miles of firm, tanned legs. "No damn way," he added.

"I'm beginning to think you're a man who leans toward stereotypes." Casually, she pulled a yellow-paper legal pad from her case before setting the bag on the floor. "I'm sorry I can't oblige you," she said as she uncapped a pen and met his gaze. "But if it's important, I can tell you that our town historical society doesn't have the cachet of nearby Charleston. They have the wealthy past, the port and the bustling tourism industry, after all. We have our own place in history—this house being one of the premier monuments, since it lasted through the War of 1812, the Civil War and countless hurricanes. We have a strong community and a need to preserve our beginnings. To respect our ancestors and all they sacrificed.

"That's all." Her bright blue eyes burned with pride. "No hidden agenda. No fund-raiser planned to lure your money into our accounts."

Maybe he'd misjudged her, and maybe he hadn't, but he refused to feel shame. There was a time when he would have considered cynicism a flaw. Now it was a vital part of life. That's what the past had done to him, stolen his openness, turned him wary and hard.

That guarded part of him spoke now, sensing that keeping her at a distance was vital. "It's good to know I won't be fleeced by you and a bunch of blue-hairs."

She wrote on her pad in a neat, looping style. Very feminine. "There's a committee of five. All volunteers. One blonde, two brunettes, a redhead and one with silver hair. The ages range from Penelope, who's sixteen, to Sister Mary Katherine, who's eighty-two. Would you like to know their qualifications?"

"No. But...*Penelope?*"

"Lovely girl. Brilliant with computers—quite a contrast to her old-fashioned name. She's digitized all our historical photos and documents. She's very shy." Her gaze met his. "And she will *not* be coming to see you."

"Why not?"

Wait. Why should he care? Why was he already picturing some tiny girl with big glasses and mousy brown hair?

"I'm sure you can guess," Sloan said, smirking.

"No, I really can't."

"You're entirely too...intense for a young girl."

Right. Of course he was. He didn't want some kid hanging

around any more than he wanted an interfering librarian smiling at him, drinking his whiskey, smelling like fruit, flowers and heaven.

She ripped off the paper she'd written on, reached into her briefcase again, then crossed the room and stuck the note to the fridge, apparently with a magnet. "This is my home phone, cell phone and e-mail address. You're going to need them as we move through the renovation process."

Who carried magnets in their briefcase? He was distracted enough by the note and the sensual sway of her hips to ask, "What else do you have in that bag?"

She turned and smiled. "All manner of things, Mr. Kendrick. You'll find I'm thorough and efficient."

"Part of the librarian code of honor?"

"Naturally."

Again, he realized she'd effortlessly made him curious about something that, fifteen minutes ago, he would have sworn wouldn't have interested him in the least.

She returned to her seat. "We really should discuss, in detail, the plans you have for Batherton House."

"My research shows it's called Batherton Mansion."

"It used to be. In its present state, I think that's a bit premature, don't you?"

He could hardly argue with that, but he leaned back in his chair and fixed her with an irritated scowl. "And yet I don't see why I should discuss, in detail, any of my plans with you."

"Didn't your lawyer explain that *all* changes to the property have to be approved by the committee?"

"Yes, but I'm not changing any of the original structure, and he told me I got approval for the paint colors, trim and light fixtures last month. Everything else is simply repairs."

"That's true." She cleared her throat. "Pardon if this sounds rude, but how do I *know* you're not changing any of the original structure unless I inspect the property on a regular basis?"

Taking my word, I guess, is too much to ask.

Thanks to the well-documented media coverage of the tragic headlines involving his family, and his own mysterious, misunderstood behavior, he could hardly blame her. But the resentment, which was mostly self-directed, burned.

He shouldn't be here with her, talking as if the past three months hadn't happened. He needed to be alone with his ghosts, fury and guilt. He didn't want her sly smiles and sparkling eyes bringing humor and lightness into the dark where he'd retreated.

Where he belonged.

And he was damned tired of feeling as if she'd taken control of everything since the moment he'd opened the door.

"Not taking the word of a crazy man?" He shifted forward, watching her eyes widen. "Despite what you read in the papers, my parents being murdered didn't send me over the edge." He almost smiled. "Not yet, anyway."

2

She let out a gasping breath.

She extended her hand and her fingers brushed across his fist, clenched on the table. "I never intended—"

When he lurched to his feet, she fell silent.

He shouldn't have brought up the ugly darkness. Why *had* he?

To be cruel? To dim that bright, clever smile? Had his family's pain and tragedy really turned him into such an unfeeling ass?

With his back to her, he forced his emotions to the pit of his stomach. "I understand you and your committee have a job to do. So do I. And I need to do it alone."

"I don't plan to burden you with my presence on a daily basis. Weekly inspections will be fine."

He suppressed a wince. "Inspections?"

"Visits," she amended.

There had to be a way around this historical accuracy nonsense. He only wanted to work and sweat, bring back elegance and beauty to *something* in this world.

"Suppose I ignore these rules? And your visits?"

"You could, I guess. But Sister Mary Katherine would consider that dishonorable, and you really don't want to get on her bad side."

Blue-hairs, teenagers, librarians and nuns were going to rule his life for the foreseeable future. It was completely, jaw-droppingly ridiculous.

"Also," Sloan added, "My daddy is the sheriff, and my granddaddy is the county judge. You *really* don't want to get on their bad side."

And the law. *Great.*

He'd seen enough cops in the last year to last a lifetime. If only her cousin was a reporter, his torture would be complete.

Heading toward the whiskey bottle, he said, "The blue-prints are in the library. Look at them all you want, make copies, pass them out to your fellow committee members, alert the media."

"Thank you. That would be helpful."

He poured his drink, then rested against the counter to sip it. "The carpenter is coming tomorrow. I'm sure you can discuss all my insidious plans with him."

"I'll be sure to do that," she said cheerfully.

"So go."

She angled her head. "Does drinking improve or sour your mood?"

"Go!"

Shrugging, not looking at all offended by his surliness, she rose from the table, then walked down the hall.

She was right. She didn't saunter. She strutted.

He poured more whiskey.

Rage and regret were living, breathing things. And both volatile. He longed to remember what his life had been like before, when his family had been happy and secure, when his communications company, which he'd inherited from his father and which had supported them all, had flourished. When he'd been full of himself and the fortunes he'd been surrounded by. When he hadn't thought being on time to dinner would be the difference between life and death. When he hadn't realized the power a total stranger had over everything that mattered.

Berating the police for lack of justice hadn't solved anything. Avoiding the media hadn't made them any less likely to go away. Selling the company hadn't soothed his grief. Working himself to exhaustion hadn't, as yet, tempered his anger.

Give it time, his friends said.

So he was.

As he sipped his drink, he forcefully pushed his thoughts to the work he'd accomplished the last few days and ignored the briefcase sitting on the floor a few feet away. He'd sanded the floor in the dining room, preparing it for staining. He'd accepted delivery of a mattress and box-spring set and assembled it into the antique mahogany bed frame he'd bought a couple of weeks ago at an estate sale. He'd repaired the bookcase in the library.

Where Sexy Sloan was now.

Why didn't she leave? Why did the sensual, tropical fruit scent of her perfume linger, even when she wasn't in the room?

He stiffened as he heard her move down the hall toward him.

"These are really good," she said, holding the rolled-up plans. "You've done a lot of work already."

"I haven't changed anything," he said sharply. "Just simple repairs."

She held up her hand. "I can see that. I saw the pictures of the new stair and balcony railing. Did you have it built?"

"I bought it at an estate sale."

"I have a hard time seeing you puttering around old houses on weekends."

He paused in the process of sipping his whiskey. "I don't putter."

"No." Her gaze drifted down his body, leaving heat and need in its wake. "I imagine you don't."

"You've got what you want," he said harshly, irritated by her ability to arouse him so effortlessly. *Now go.*

She seemed to sense his unspoken words and crossed to her briefcase, which she set on the kitchen table. "I'll get the plans back to you tomorrow."

"Fine."

Straightening, she faced him. "I'm not your enemy, Aidan."

It was the first time she'd called him by his given name, and the moment sent a pulse of excitement through his veins. A moment he didn't want and shouldn't feel.

"I'm sorry about your parents," she added.

He never knew what to say to this. *Thanks? They lived a long and full life?* Since neither of those were true, he remained silent.

Hitching her briefcase on her shoulder, she started out. "It's a nice town. You'll be—"

"Happy?" He shook his head. "I want to be alone."

"I was going to say you'll be accepted," she said softly. "If you make an effort."

"I want to be alone."

"Yeah?" She cocked her head, her eyes bright with challenge. "How's that workin' out for you so far?"

He tossed back the rest of his whiskey. "Fine," he lied.

With a half smile, she nodded. "I'll leave you to it." She turned and headed down the hall and toward the front door.

Finally.

And yet some mad, invisible force pulled him after her.

Watching her hips sway as she walked, he reflected on times when he'd been whole and happy. He used to run a successful, international communications company. He used to wear custom-made designer suits and attend all the important events in Atlanta. He used to be sociable. He used to relish the attention of smart, beautiful women like Sloan.

Today, the shell of him that walked through the dark, dusty halls of this ancient house had consumed him.

But wasn't it right that he was here? Hadn't his thoughtless attitude put his parents in danger? Hadn't his failure to see the cold world realistically reminded him in a brutal way that he had to embrace darkness to see it clearly?

Didn't he *deserve* to be alone?

She brushed her fingers across his cheek. "Where'd you go?"

Unnerved by her touch, by the tenderness in her expressive blue eyes, he jerked back. "Nowhere pleasant."

She sighed, as if exasperated by his continual—yet completely failing—efforts at distance. "When was the last time you had a decent meal?"

He thought of the ham sandwich he'd had for dinner. "Define *decent*."

"I'll bring you something from Mabel's Café for lunch tomorrow. Along with returning your plans," she added quickly, as if sensing the protest that rose to his lips. "My apology for showing up unannounced tonight. Besides, if you're going to work yourself into the ground, you need nourishment. If you get sick, you can't work."

Since he could think of no immediate argument to that, he nodded. "Fine."

There was a lot of fineness going on, actually. And none of it on his part.

As they talked, he'd been keeping his gaze focused—deliberately—on her face, but now he let it slip over her curves, her long, seemingly endless legs.

Merciful heaven.

His whole body, already aroused, hardened like steel. He

wanted her beyond sense and reason, beyond his self-imposed isolation. Certainly beyond what he deserved.

"Do you get a lot of teenage boys hanging out at the library?"

Since she was halfway down the steps when he spoke, she had to glance over her shoulder to look at him. She smiled, no doubt completely aware of the effect she had on the male population. "They're my best customers."

"SORRY TO DRAG all of you down here so early," Sloan began, glancing around the library's conference table at her fellow committee members. "But I felt we should get on top of this project immediately."

It was 7:00 a.m. on Tuesday, the only time everyone could gather before work and school to discuss the all-important restoration of Aidan's house.

"Batherton Mansion could be a jewel for us," said Courtney, a fiery redhead who owned the local hair and nail salon.

"If we can get Kendrick to cooperate," Helen, their local real-estate agent added. "I've dealt with him, and only through his attorney, but this guy is tough."

"But he obviously cares about history," Penelope pointed out, blinking behind her large steel-framed glasses. "Why else would he buy this house over some posh and trendy beachside resort?"

"We don't have posh and trendy," Helen said.

Penelope nodded. "Exactly. He probably wants peace and quiet." She lowered her voice. "Especially after being chased by reporters for the last few months."

"And that's precisely the problem, ladies." Sister Mary Katherine folded her hands in front of her. "We simply can't have our reputation gaining at the expense of Mr. Kendrick. He's been through enough."

"Still, we have to attract some new members to the committee," Helen reminded them. "Rich ones, if possible."

"Or a corporate sponsor," Courtney said. "We can't let the few historical properties we have fall into disrepair. Not after all *we've* been through."

Looking uncertain, Penelope bit her lip.

Sloan, being the lone member who'd actually encountered the prickly former executive, who'd obviously longed to throw her bodily from his precious house, tended to lean toward Helen and Courtney's side. She sympathized with his grief, but the committee had its own problems.

She was also annoyed that she lusted after the man.

And she was trying desperately to hide it.

"We just want to put his house on our brochure to attract more tourists and new members in the area, not exploit his personal life." Helen continued, "And wouldn't it be nice to hold a fund-raiser out there when everything's finished? Sort of an elegant wine-and-cheese party?"

"Or a tea," Courtney suggested. "With those sweet little biscuits Mabel makes."

Sloan frowned. "That's going to be tricky. I specifically told him we were neither using him for a fund-raiser nor after his money."

"We're not using *him*," Helen insisted. "We're using the house."

"Though if he wanted to make a sizable donation," Courtney added, "we certainly wouldn't say no."

"But isn't one of our goals more media exposure?" Penelope asked, as always, wise beyond her years. "If we call attention to Batherton Mansion, it will naturally call attention to the owner. I don't think Mr. Kendrick is interested in any more TV or newspaper coverage."

"Perhaps after we get to know Mr. Kendrick a bit better," Sister Mary Katherine offered, "we'll feel more comfortable asking for his help in raising our profile in the area."

Sloan didn't think it was appropriate to share with the nun just how *well* she wanted to get to know Aidan Kendrick, so she remained silent and let the discussion buzz around her.

She couldn't imagine losing her father so tragically, then having her life and business practices scrutinized on a daily basis. Maybe Aidan Kendrick could have handled things better—a few well-timed, but brief statements.

Instead, he'd tried to hide, and that only made the reporters more determined to uncover the dirt he was concealing. Did reckless playboy Aidan Kendrick owe money to the mob? Were his parents' supposed mugging and murders really payback? Was he into drugs and had crossed the wrong dealer? Had he dated a woman with a jealous boyfriend—or even a husband?

The police had discounted all these wild theories and called the case a simple mugging, but Kendrick had kept quiet, so they persisted. He'd sold his successful company, disappeared for a month, then, a couple of weeks ago, wound up on tiny Palmer's Island.

She didn't want to cause the man more problems, but if the committee didn't do something quickly, if they couldn't attract more members and their funds, they'd likely lose the historical properties they owned and maintained.

Though they'd had a lucrative budget to buy the first church established on the island and a historical home once owned by a pirate, several of their benefactors had passed away in the last few years. Those properties needed constant maintenance, payment of water and power bills and a staff of tour guides.

To keep the revenue coming in for those expenses, they had

to attract new tourists to their area and sign up a whole bunch of new, dues-paying members. A really rich benefactor would be a dream come true, hence the interest in both Aidan's property and Aidan himself.

"I think we should call for a vote," Sloan said after a few minutes.

She, Helen and Courtney carried the motion three to two. "So, we plan to use Batherton Mansion in our next publicity campaign. And, ladies, let's keep this between us for now. We're going to need to approach Mr. Kendrick slowly and carefully."

"And make sure we can protect his identity," Penelope said, with concern.

"Naturally," Sloan said easily.

Approaching Aidan with this idea now would never work. In his present state, there was no way he would be open to photographers and historians tramping through his precious halls.

The ways she might soften him up flitted through her mind, heating her blood, sending anticipation soaring.

She cleared her throat and forced her attention back to business. "Now, what do all of you think of the plans?"

They discussed the various materials and styles Aidan was using and all agreed they were aesthetically superior, as well as historically accurate. The fact that this house would soon be returned to its glory, and on their little island, was exciting and encouraging.

When the meeting broke up, Penelope and Sister Mary Katherine walked out the door together and Helen took the opportunity to grab Sloan's arm and hold her back. "So, how hot is he?"

Courtney, brown eyes sparkling with interest, leaned in to hear all the good stuff.

Remembering the wicked heat that flared intermittently in Aidan's silver eyes, the silky-looking texture of his inky hair and his long, lean body, Sloan barely suppressed a shudder of longing. And since both women were always on top of the latest island gossip, she didn't see any point in lying. "Off the scale."

They groaned simultaneously.

Sloan could hardly argue that reaction.

"Since you got there first, I guess this means he's off-limits to the rest of us," Helen said.

"You *are* the mankiller in this town," Courtney added, then grinned.

Sloan stared at her. "I am *not*." Well, maybe lately she had been dating quite a bit. When a girl was unceremoniously dumped, she was entitled.

Courtney's gaze turned speculative. "Your ego and heart aren't still bruised over Davis, are they?"

Knowing she definitely didn't want that nugget dropping around town, Sloan crossed her arms over her chest and made an effort to look bored. *"Please."*

Helen leaned her shoulder against the door frame. "Oh, so you're not upset he's back in town?"

Sloan swallowed hard. Her susceptible, traitorous heart thumped with almost painful intensity. "He's back?" she managed to ask, suddenly realizing Helen had been dying to share this information for the last half hour.

"Definitely," Helen replied.

Courtney shrugged. "He worked for Kendrick Communications, which has now been sold. There was bound to be some fallout with the employees."

Again, Sloan couldn't help but think Aidan and Davis in the same town wasn't a coincidence. Were the two men friends? Davis, for all his faults, had been an islander his whole life. She supposed he'd mentioned his hometown to his boss at some point.

"I'm sure Davis will come looking for you," Helen said, her smile sly. "You'll give us all the details when he does, won't you?"

"Sure. You bet," Sloan agreed absently, still trying to wrap her mind around the idea that Davis was on Palmer's Island.

What was he doing here?

There was no doubt he could land a job with another big-time company in Atlanta. Returning to his roots was a step backward.

Not to mention her daddy still had vague ideas about rein-stituting the firing squad for the sin of Davis hurting and hu-miliating his precious daughter.

She said good-bye to Helen and Courtney, then headed to the main desk to actually start doing her job. She reorganized the entire medieval research area, dusted seventeenth-century fiction and helped two students find the history of bacteria and antibiotics for the science fair.

But the whole time, she thought of Helen's news.

Davis is here.

He could be standing on the front steps even now. He might have left her a message—she checked her cell phone six times. He could drop by her condo at any moment.

Davis, with his charming smile, sandy-blond hair and cheerful elegance was a polar opposite to dark and brooding Aidan Kendrick. Was that *why* she was so attracted to Aidan? Was she subconsciously leaning toward a man totally unlike the one who'd broken her heart and left her beloved island for more excitement and another woman?

At eleven-thirty, one of the Junior League volunteers arrived, so Sloan quickly made copies of Aidan's plans, then headed toward the café. There, she took Mabel's advice and ordered two blue plate specials—country-fried steak with sawmill gravy, collard greens, creamed corn and hot yeast rolls. And, of course, sweet tea.

Hey, it wasn't part of the low-carb, low-fat diet, but it was comforting.

As she pulled into the driveway at Aidan's, she checked her cell phone again—though it hadn't rung. If Davis *was* here, why hadn't he called?

Her mind half on historical society business and half on Davis, she wasn't paying too much attention to the door she'd knocked on.

Until it opened.

Aidan stood in the opening. Luscious and beautiful, even with his fierce scowl.

The stubble on his face was slightly thicker. She wanted to stroke it as much as she wanted to see that magnificent jaw clean-shaven. He wore a snug navy T-shirt, showing off his lean torso and leanly muscled arms, and she couldn't help but wonder about the heat and feel of the skin the shirt covered.

"I'm trying to work here," he said rudely.

Her gaze darted up to his. *Wow, oh, wow.* He did have those intense eyes. Davis's eyes were a nice, safe, sort-of-boring brown.

Then the scent of Mabel's special hit her.

"I brought lunch. Like I said." Sloan held up the bag. "You have time for a break now?"

His eyes flashed with irritation. "No."

In her other hand, she held up his original plans. "I'm also returning these."

He took the rolled-up plans and considered her. "That does smell good."

Okay, note to self—don't attempt to seduce the hot, new guy with perfume.

She smiled. "Uh-huh."

He sighed and stepped back, allowing her to enter.

"I'm assuming you have candles and wine at the ready," she said breezily—if sarcastically—as she walked inside.

"I don't."

"No?" She turned, giving him a purposefully surprised look. "I told you that I'd bring you lunch today, so I assumed you'd be expecting me." She paused. "Or at least grateful that I showed up to feed you."

He remained silent. A muscle along his jaw pulsed. Finally, he extended his arm toward the hallway leading to the kitchen. "So feed me."

Her first instinct was to dump Mabel's special gravy over his head, but she resisted the urge and reminded herself that she wasn't much for accepting help, either.

She was her father's daughter, and she could handle anything that came her way. With her mother gone, surrounded by lawmen, the sisters at the Catholic school where she attended were her primary female influences. So, she'd developed the strength and ruthless nature of men and the compassion and sense of community responsibility that taught her to work, not take handouts.

Without commenting, she pulled the plastic food containers from the bag. "I brought napkins and utensils. I wasn't sure if you had them."

"I have forks and paper towels."

"Metal forks?"

"Plastic."

"Naturally." She finished laying out the meal and tried to pretend her pulse wasn't vibrating simply from the sound of his voice. "I must say, Mr. Kendrick, this is by far the fanciest date I've been on in months."

"This isn't a date."

She dropped into a chair and looked up to see him scowling at her, as usual. "You're telling me." Smiling, she patted the chair next to her. "You're hungry. Have a seat."

He hesitated.

She met his gaze. "I'm not going to keep asking."

He sat.

They ate in silence for several minutes. "This is good," he said, somehow sounding impressed and reluctant at the same time. "I was starving."

"You can't do the work you want without rest and fuel."

"Is that a speech?"

She paused and looked over at him as she sipped her tea. "Are speeches usually one-liners?"

"I guess not."

"Then, no, that wasn't a speech."

After several more minutes passed, she rose, folding her napkin, dumping her empty plate into the large, gray plastic can he'd so artfully set near the back door. When she turned back, he was standing behind her.

All six-foot-three amazing inches of him.

She drew a quick breath. Her gaze jumped to his. "Your eyes are bloodshot."

"Up too late last night."

Since his body heat was making her head spin, she simply took his plate from him and dumped it into the trash.

When she turned back, he was close.

Really close.

"Thank you," he said, his gaze roving her face.

"You're welcome."

He scowled. "I thought about *you* half the night."

Her stomach quivered. "That's a bad thing?"

"Yes."

This negative attitude toward her was really starting to be annoying. Unrequited lust wasn't familiar territory for her. And though Aidan obviously wasn't totally immune to her, her ego was taking a pretty serious hit. Why was she bringing him lunch, trying to make conversation, sympathizing with his pain and, in general, being nice, when his only genuine smile probably came the moment the door shut behind her?

She lifted her chin. "Well, that's just f—"

His lips captured hers, silencing her in a flash. Her heart jumped in her chest, and she was pretty sure she let out a moan of longing, then she angled her head and sank into him.

He didn't hesitate to tangle his tongue with hers. He tasted of the lemon he drank with his tea. He smelled of sawdust and spicy sandalwood.

She clutched his T-shirt in her fist, grasping to get closer, to absorb him into her. She wanted to feel his bare, sleek skin against hers, to have that intense gaze focused on her, to feel his muscles harden beneath her…to have him tremble and gasp along with her.

His hands, braced at the lower part of her back, molded her to his body, and she felt his need, the hunger, the wild lust. It had been a long time, too long, since she'd felt desire grab her so effectively by the throat. Since the liquid heat of her body had rushed and pulsed.

She wasn't sure she'd ever felt so—

Ding-dong.

Aidan lifted his head, his eyes flashing silver like a wolf after prey. "What the devil is that?"

"Doorbell," Sloan gasped, linking her hands behind his

head, tugging him back to her, inhaling the sharp scent of arousal. "They'll go away."

Their mouths met again. He nipped her bottom lip with his teeth. Light and gloriously exciting. She wanted—

Ding-dong, ding-dong.

He yanked away, looked down at her and snarled.

Okay, maybe I'm taking this wolf metaphor a little too far...

"I'm going to kill whoever's at the door." He stalked away, apparently to do just that.

Sort of curious but mostly to cheer him on, Sloan followed him, pausing at the end of the hall, from where she could see the front door, but avoid the more serious bloodshed.

She *did* have on her favorite cream pantsuit, after all.

"What the hell do you want?" Aidan barked.

Again with the metaphor.

Sloan shook her head, sure the other voice was a man's. And familiar.

"She's busy," Aidan said. "Come back later." He started to close the door.

A hand gripped the edge of the door, forcing it open. "Where is she?"

Sloan gasped. That sounded like—

Davis, his hair lighter, his face paler than she remembered, appeared in the doorway. His head swiveled right and left, then he caught sight of her, hovering in the hall.

"Hey, baby," he said, smiling as he started toward her. "Miss me?"

3

BABY.

What a common, stupid name. Especially for Sloan.

Sloan Caldwell was no baby. For one, there was nothing cute about her. She had smoldering looks, hot legs and amazing, erotic lips.

But Aidan watched—with no small amount of resentment—as his former sales manager, Davis Curnan, slid his arms around the woman *he'd* been holding only moments before and lifted her off her feet for a hug.

"You look beautiful, as always," Davis said, setting her down and cupping her cheek.

Sloan smiled, though a little hesitantly. "Thanks."

The whole reunion made Aidan's stomach turn—and not just because he wanted Sloan for himself. Last time he'd checked, Davis had been dating a brunette from his accounting department.

"As heartwarming as all this is," he began, walking slowly in their direction, barely resisting the urge to grab Davis and shove him out the door, "I'm afraid the lunch break is over."

Sloan's gaze shot to him, as if she'd forgotten he was there. *Great.* Now he was forgettable.

"Oh, Aidan. Ah—" She glanced at Davis, then wriggled out of his arms. "I guess you know Davis."

"Of course," Davis said, then smiled. "He used to sign my paychecks."

Aidan raised his eyebrows. "Actually, they were processed in the *accounting* department, if you recall."

Davis found humility long enough to act embarrassed. "Right." His gaze slid to Sloan. "Not anymore."

Ah, so the big-city romance is over, and now you've come back to claim the small-town girl.

Aidan had known, of course, that his sales manager was from Palmer's Island. In fact, the few conversations they'd had about Davis's hometown had led him to investigate the area for real estate after his parents' deaths and his need for a new beginning. Davis could technically be termed responsible for Aidan's coming to the island.

Davis's involvement with Sloan, however, was a nasty surprise Aidan didn't like one little bit.

"We have a lot to catch up on," Davis cajoled, sliding his hand to the small of Sloan's back. "Why don't we let Aidan get back to work, darling?"

"Darling?" Sloan's expression went from pleasantly embarrassed to seriously pissed in the space of a heartbeat. She grabbed his hand and flung it off her. "You ran out on me, dumped me for somebody else and now you dare come back here over six months later, calling me *baby* and *darling,* thinking I'm gonna jump into your arms?" She narrowed her eyes. "Think again."

Feeling much better, Aidan rocked back on his heels, dying to see how the clever salesman would slide his way out of this tight spot.

Davis turned bright red. "Sloan, honey—I don't really think this is the place—"

"Sure it is. You came here to find me." She held out her arms. "Here I am."

Davis actually winced. Aidan had never seen him so rattled. But then fury from a goddess like Sloan was bound to put any man off his stride. Hadn't Aidan himself spent half the night debating whether he should put his efforts into seducing her or running in the opposite direction?

"Aidan," Davis said, turning toward him. "Would you mind giving us some privacy to settle this?"

Aidan leaned boldly against the rickety stairway railing he was due to replace that week. "I'm fine right here."

"That chick you dumped me for worked for him, didn't she?" Sloan asked, her voice vibrating with anger. "What was her name?"

"Rebecca," Aidan supplied—with more cheer than maybe he should have.

He wished he didn't relish this confrontation so much, but that warm hug between Davis and Sloan, coming just after his and Sloan's incredible kiss, had jolted him with jealousy.

Five minutes ago, he'd simply wanted time to wrestle with his demons and consider assuaging some of his loneliness in Sloan's arms. Now, suddenly, if he wanted her, he was too late. And, regardless, he might not have a prayer of her wanting him anyway.

The ex had arrived.

"This isn't about her," Davis said, facing Sloan, turning his back on Aidan.

"Oh?" Sloan looked surprised. "You haven't come to announce your engagement? Invite me to the wedding? Have a quick roll between the sheets before you commit?"

"There's no wedding." Sighing, Davis attempted to steer Sloan out of the foyer, but she simply shook her head and crossed her arms over her chest. "Things between Rebecca and I were never quite right," he said quietly after a quick, embarrassed glance back at Aidan. "I only broke it off with you because I was tired of our long-distance relationship."

"It was *your* idea to go work in Atlanta in the first place."

"What was I supposed to do? Take over my dad's insurance office? Hang around boring Palmer's Island all my life?"

Sloan's eyes flashed dangerously. "Yes."

"Well, I wasn't ready to do that." He rolled his shoulders. "However, things change. I realized I made a mistake."

"You've been gone for months, Davis. It took you quite a while to work out that mistake."

"It was okay at first. I was happy, and I thought you were probably better off, too. We needed to see other people, find out what else was out there."

Sloan glanced down, but not quickly enough that Aidan failed to see the hurt in her eyes. "I didn't."

"I'm sorry." He laid his fingers under her chin and lifted her head. "I screwed up."

"Did she break up with you?"

"No." He stroked her arm. "Things just kind of…fell apart."

"Got boring?" she challenged.

Davis shrugged. "I don't know. I only know I missed you."

"Convenient that this missing me started after Aidan sold the company."

"I missed you before that."

The simple explanation and clear sentiment behind it was hard to argue with. Sloan obviously felt the same, since she didn't protest.

"I got back to the island last night," he added, "and couldn't wait to see you."

Sloan moved away from him, wandering around the foyer. "I heard."

"Already?"

"Gossip is the only thing that travels fast in this town. Helen told me this—" She whirled toward him. "Why did you come *here?* To this house? In another fifteen minutes I would have been back at the library."

Or in my bed. And Aidan wished like hell he'd taken Sloan's advice and ignored the door, forcing the intruder to go away.

Again, Davis glanced at Aidan. "I did go to the library. The clerk said you were here with the new owner, who turned out to be Aidan. So I decided to come right over."

Now that was interesting, Aidan thought. Davis obviously hadn't rushed over with a housewarming gift. Was it possible Davis considered him a threat to his big, happy reunion plans?

To complicate matters, he and Davis had had some minor wars over business decisions in the past. While he respected the other man's understanding of sales and dealing with customer issues, his overall marketing strategy was too impulsive and not clearly defined. If not for his family tragedy, Aidan was sure he would have eventually fired Davis.

Was this trip back home another impulse?

Should he share these observations with Sloan? Or was he simply feeling his own level of threat from the easygoing ex?

And why was he getting so worked up about a woman he'd known less than twenty-four hours? Why did he care if she and Davis made up, screwed themselves silly, then settled into cheery, small-town life? Why did he care if Davis got his hands on that luscious body, those lips that—

Hell.

"I'm going back to work," he said, stalking through the foyer.

"No," Sloan said, stepping into his path, placing her hand

on his chest. "Davis should go." She glanced at him. "Aidan and I have things to discuss."

Davis's gaze moved to Sloan's hand, then back to her face. "Discuss?"

"About the renovations."

"I can discuss renovations."

"Please go, Davis," she said emphatically.

Davis opened his mouth, no doubt prepared to argue.

"Don't worry," Aidan couldn't resist saying with a fierce look at his former employee. "I'll take good care of her."

Davis glared at him. "I just bet you will." He turned to Sloan. "I'll call you," he said in a gentle tone.

One he no doubt practiced on a daily basis.

"Fine," she said coolly.

Davis let himself out of the house.

"What a mess!" Sloan burst out the moment the door closed, throwing up her hands. "Our relationship was always out of balance. Why that man, of all the others, could always hit me right here—" she tapped her chest "—I'll never understand."

"*All* the others?"

Still ranting, Sloan seemed not to hear him. "The down-right, outrageous nerve of him, thinking I'd jump for orgasmic joy at the sight of him."

"Orgasmic?" Even as the idea sent ripples of anticipation through his body, she rolled on.

"I wonder if he expected to have to apologize right away, or if he thought I'd fall onto my back immediately."

"He acted sincere," Aidan said, shrugging. "But who knows?"

"A bit slick and convenient, but, I guess, sincere." She stopped, then waved her hand and continued pacing.

Whether she was brushing aside the slickness or the sincerity, Aidan wasn't sure. Her anger at Davis was good enough for him. His competitive nature was one of the qualities that had helped him to run his company so effectively.

He'd spent last night resisting Sloan. Was he now going to give in simply to win?

The idea troubled him as much as it excited him.

It had been a long time since he'd been excited.

As the arguments rushed through his head, he watched her move. She'd taken to pacing in circles. His body throbbed, watching her hips sway. When she flipped her hair over her shoulder, he groaned silently, barely resisting the urge to bury his fingers in the silky strands. Imagining those blond locks cascading across his stomach as she moved—

"I'm sorry about all that," she said as she approached him, startling him out of his fantasy.

"It was—" He made an effort to think about hammering. Well, no, that wasn't good. He concentrated on the image of sweeping. Sweeping, like her hair would brush across his body, tickling, *arousing*… "—no problem," he somehow managed to say.

"I shouldn't have pulled you into the middle of the argument. I'm sure you felt awkward."

Since she was close enough now to touch, he concentrated on her face, though he found that equally distracting. "I enjoyed myself mostly. My personal favorite moment was when you mocked him about his pet names for you."

"Mmm." She smiled with remembrance. "I was working on the fly, but I thought that had a nice touch of anger and disbelief."

"It did."

"May I ask you a question?"

"Why stop now?" he asked, though the sarcasm didn't have the same heat it might have had last night. That insane, amazing kiss had broken down a barrier he didn't think he wanted to reconstruct, even if he could.

"Davis worked for you," she said. "Did you not like him?"

"I did until he started ringing my damn doorbell."

Her gaze connected with his. Fire lit with blue flames. "His timing was never that great."

"Never?" He lifted the corners of his mouth and lowered his tone. "There are moments when timing is essential."

Her gaze dropped to his lips. "There certainly are."

Ding-dong.

Sloan groaned. "You've got to be kidding. If that's him again, I'm gonna—" She flung open the door. "Oh, hey, Pete."

Pete Willis, wearing an orange-and-white ball cap, worn jeans and a blue cotton shirt, stood on the porch. As Sloan stepped back, he walked inside, carrying an armload of tools. Despite the fact that he was barely twenty, he was reputed to be the best carpenter in town. So far, Aidan had to agree.

"Hey, Miss Caldwell." He nodded at Aidan. "I'm a few minutes early, Mr. Kendrick. That all right?"

Hell, no. "Sure," Aidan said, wondering if he could squeeze in a cold shower before getting back to work. "Why don't you check out the supplies in the parlor? I'll be right there."

He laid his hand on Sloan's lower back and ushered her onto the porch. "Thanks again for lunch."

"Anytime." She lifted her hand as if she might touch him, then let it fall by her side. "Sorry about my personal drama."

"It's fine. Thanks for returning the plans."

She nodded. "I promised I would." Pausing, she added, "I always keep my promises."

He didn't. Though he'd wanted to.

He hadn't taken care of his family, his greatest responsibility. Was that why he felt such an intense need to be with this woman, even as he felt guilty for being alive at all? Lately he'd barely spoken to anyone, much less made an effort to pursue the company of a woman for conversation, a dinner companion or sex. But there was *something* about Sloan. Why? What made her so special?

Maybe he was just lonely.

Which had to be what prompted him to ask, "When do you think you'll need to come back for another inspection?"

"When do you want me back?"

Oh, boy. He didn't want her to leave. "You're welcome anytime."

She raised her eyebrows. "Am I really? How's Friday night? We could have dinner this time."

That's three days away. "Okay," he found himself saying. "Sounds good." *And when did I turn into such a lame idiot?* "All I can make is ham sandwiches and spaghetti," he added in a stronger tone. "If you want something else, you'll have to make it."

"Hey." She stepped so close her breasts brushed his chest. "Don't go back to being captain of Team Surly just yet. I happen to like spaghetti."

He was actually encouraging company. The concept had been so foreign over the last few months, he was amazed he was taking the step. He wasn't going to go crazy and actually get out and socialize, but if he was trying to heal his battered spirit, dinner with a hot blonde might be a promising start.

"Then that's what we'll have," he said.

She angled her head. "You're not inviting me to dinner just to tick off Davis, are you?"

"No. Of course not." He grinned. "Though that's a side benefit."

She took a step back so suddenly, he grabbed her around her waist. "What? Too honest? Look, I—"

She raised on her toes and pressed her mouth—lightly—to his. "Not at all. You just have a really nice smile."

THE MEMORY of Aidan's breathtaking smile followed Sloan around like an arc of sunshine all week long. If the man suddenly got cheerful on her, she might have to give the renovation project to somebody else, someone unsusceptible to his allure, since she would find it impossible to talk in his presence.

Sister Mary Katherine was her first choice. And, even for her, that smile was bound to be an issue.

Besides, she could enjoy Aidan and still do her job objectively. She wanted to see where that wildly hot kiss of theirs would go if it was repeated and uninterrupted. And if he smiled and backed her against the wall, pressing that leanly muscular body to hers, she wouldn't complain.

Would she?

As she packed her briefcase and prepared to lock up the library for the day, her thoughts turned from her upcoming date to Davis.

He'd been calling, of course, but she was playing it cool with him. Now that the initial shock was past, and her anger had somewhat abated, she'd been dwelling on her devastation and humiliation at his leaving in the first place. She'd thought he'd been The One. The one who'd be her love-of-a-lifetime, the relationship her parents had had.

But he'd left, and she'd sealed off her heart.

Now, he was suddenly back because he'd missed her?

She'd love to know what had really happened between him and that chick he'd been seeing in Atlanta. Maybe she'd left him for somebody else. He'd said she hadn't broken up with him, but she could have left without notice and sent a note later. That wasn't a breakup; it was abandonment.

She ought to know.

Mostly, she kept waiting for the other shoe to drop, for him to tell her he wanted something from her. Or, worse, for there to be no shoe at all. For him to dart back to Atlanta, or wherever, leaving his small-town roots behind. Again.

Focusing on Aidan was much more pleasurable.

So without effort, she put aside her worries about Davis and left the library to get ready for her date.

She'd hit Aidan with her LBD the first time they'd met, so she debated between something similar or contrasting. Maybe she should go with jeans, a flowy top and wedge heels. Casual sexy. Or she could go all out with a stop-sign-red dress. Obvious sexy. Or a feminine, springlike dress and straw hat. Picnic sexy.

Or was that too Scarlett O'Hara?

Good grief, romance was complicated.

She settled on the jeans outfit. After gathering her purse and the bread and salad ingredients she'd agreed to bring, she headed toward Aidan's house. He was supposed to do the spaghetti and provide wine, which she needed, if the nervous fluttering in her stomach was any guide.

When she reached the porch, she noticed there were lighted sconces by the door and that the lower porch railing had been replaced. Obviously, Aidan and Pete had been working hard the last few days.

Batherton House was a typical Charleston-style double house with both first- and second-floor porches that dominated the front of the house. The central hallway separated the house, with rooms on either side. In the days before air conditioning, this allowed for better ventilation. There were some historic homes in downtown Charleston that still didn't have full central air, but they were museums. Sloan and her fellow committee members were so thrilled to see the house coming alive again, that they certainly weren't going to argue about an absolutely necessary mechanism for comfort in steamy South Carolina.

Thinking of steamy, she immediately thought of Aidan. A bead of sweat rolled down her back into the waistband of her jeans. She waved her hand in front of her face. Maybe she should have worn the skirt.

After ringing the doorbell, she forced herself to think enticing and positive thoughts and planted a bright smile on her face.

Which faded when Pete opened the door.

She glanced at her watch, though she knew it was just after seven o'clock. "Ah…hey, Pete," she said, looking over his shoulder and hoping to see Aidan.

But she didn't.

Pete stepped back, inviting her inside. "Hey, Miss Caldwell. I was closer to the door, so Mr. Kendrick asked me to answer it."

She adjusted the grocery bag on her hip. "Oh."

She was so insignificant as a date that not only was he not ready for her arrival, he also had his handyman playing butler? Why did she always manage to find the insensitive—

"Sorry, I'm not ready," Aidan said, walking quickly toward her from the other end of the hall and wiping his hands on a cloth. "Pete and I were finishing up and lost track of time." He took the bag from her hands.

His face glistened with sweat; his dark hair curled across his forehead. Stubble shadowed his jaw. He looked, as always, alluring, strong and delicious.

Her annoyance vanished.

Was that weak? Probably.

"I'm going," Pete said. "I'll get my stuff." He grinned. "I have a hot date myself."

When he wandered into the parlor, Sloan asked Aidan, "Between us, am I the hot date, or are you?"

"Definitely you. I'm sweaty."

"I could start making the salad while you shower."

Leaning toward her, he smiled that amazing smile, his eyes lighting with sensual sparks. "Or you could join me."

4

SLOAN let her gaze glide over the planes of Aidan's body.

Tempting?

Definitely.

Still, that luscious package came with a whole lotta baggage.

"That's quite presumptuous of you, Mr. Kendrick," she said, though she slid the tip of her finger down his broad chest as she spoke. "I think I'll make the salad instead."

She took the bag back from him and headed toward the kitchen. Behind her, she heard the murmurs of Aidan's and Pete's voices.

As she grew closer, the scent of spaghetti sauce washed over her. Clearly, Aidan had been doing something besides hammering all day.

She set her bag on the counter, then crossed to the stove, lifting off the stock-pot lid and inhaling deeply. She recognized lots of oregano, basil and garlic. A man who knew his history and his sauces was pretty much irresistible.

As she pulled lettuce, tomatoes and cucumbers from the grocery bag, she also noted that her name and phone numbers were still hanging on the fridge door and found it oddly comforting that he'd saved them. Smiling, she pulled out the wide-rimmed wooden bowl she'd brought along with the food.

"You brought a bowl?"

She glanced over her shoulder as Aidan approached. "And silverware and wineglasses. Your provisions are sparse, as I recall."

"Were sparse." He opened a drawer beside her, revealing brand-new silverware. "Already been through the dishwasher and everything. Plus…" He swung open a cabinet beside the sink. "New dishes. The ceramic kind. And wineglasses." He reached into another cabinet and pulled out two, setting them on the counter.

She batted her lashes. "All for little ol' me?"

"Yes."

He looked so pleased with himself, her breath caught. If the man was going to start being charming, she was in big trouble.

You're already in big trouble.

"Sorry I wasn't ready when you got here," he said, moving closer. "We were on a roll today."

She swallowed as her heart rate picked up speed. "The banister to the stairs is up."

His silver eyes flashed with pleasure. "You noticed."

"Of course. It's beautiful."

"It makes a difference. The other railing was rickety, possibly dangerous, and now it looks finished."

"And welcoming," she said.

He drew his brows together. "Welcoming, huh? You don't think people will want to come over and look at it, do you?"

Charm was clearly a brief and impulsive state for him. The man was warily unsociable in the extreme. "Gee, wouldn't that be horrible?"

"Yes." His gaze searched hers. "Really, it's only your opinion that matters."

Seriously? She smiled. Maybe she was making an impression. Maybe—

"Because of your connection to the historical committee," he added.

Then again, maybe not. "Of course."

Yet he'd invited her to dinner. He was obviously attracted to her. He was certainly interested in her. Whether he liked her—or anybody else—was another subject entirely.

He'd been through a traumatic time lately. Parents' deaths. Violent crime. Media frenzy. They were bound to throw even the strongest off stride. And she suspected Aidan was the one who usually threw others off balance.

As did she.

He was a loner. If not before, certainly now. And she was very sociable. Between her dad, her friends, her work and her committees, she was rarely alone.

But she liked being alone with him.

She had no desire to go to a crowded restaurant or music-blasting club. She was content with spaghetti at his kitchen table.

Maybe they weren't so far apart after all. But was that a good thing?

She fought for a casual tone. "So I'll start on the salad while you take your shower."

"Okay." His gaze roved her face for a second before he said, "I haven't done this in a while."

"Showered or eaten?"

He laughed. Actually, laughed. Her body went hot and tingly. *Oh, boy.* She was in big, big trouble.

"Had a date," he said lightly, while she scrambled to remember the dark, angry man she'd met less than a week ago.

"I bet it comes back to you."

His lips tipped up at the corners. "I hope so."

After he left, she began assembling the salad—and thinking hard about the step they were taking.

It's a simple date. What's the big deal?

Simple. Of course. Yet it didn't feel uncomplicated or straightforward.

She still sensed his pain, forced right beneath the surface, hovering there and waiting for a chance to spring. And while part of her wanted to know the real story behind the speculation about him, part of her didn't care. She sort of wanted him to talk about his family and what had driven him to change his life so drastically, but in some ways it didn't matter. She wanted to know who he was now. She wanted to live only in the moment.

The sexual tension between them was palpable. If that kiss the other day was any kind of guide, their chemistry was incredible. Did she really want to complicate things with deep conversations about suppressed feelings?

No. She really didn't. Chemistry was welcome. Heat was enough.

Besides, with Davis back in town, she had drama and emotional confusion all on her own.

By the time Aidan returned, she'd opened and poured the wine. And crammed her worries into the back of her mind.

"The sauce is ready," he announced. "All we have to do is boil the pasta."

"Good. I'm starving." She handed him a glass of wine, her pulse skipping a beat. He smelled of musk, oak and sandalwood, and his hair was still damp, jet-black waves brushing his forehead. "When did you have time to make sauce today?"

"I took a break around three." He leaned against the counter next to her. "Are you impressed by my talents in the kitchen?"

She sipped wine to ease her dry throat. She was sure he had talents in lots of areas. "Very."

He raised his glass to her. "You like the wine?"

"It doesn't have the burn of whiskey."

"Subtlety is better sometimes." He glanced at the liquor bottle, sitting several inches away. "Wine suits my mood better tonight."

Did that mean he was going to stop scowling at her? Did that mean the pain of whatever was driving him to whiskey the other night had eased?

Did she really want answers to either of those questions?

"Show me what you did today," she said lightly, once again ignoring any thoughts that led to complex conversations and hidden emotions.

As they headed out of the kitchen, he asked, "Is this my official visit for the week?"

"I think this is about my third visit this week. I'm already breaking my word to not become a nuisance."

He captured her hand and squeezed. "You're not. I like having you here."

She stopped and stared at him. "You do?"

He frowned, looking as surprised by his admittance as she felt. "Sure."

"I thought you wanted to brood alone in your dark and scary castle."

Tugging her hand, he led her into the foyer. "You'll have me as the lead in a gothic novel pretty soon."

"Pretty soon? I'm already there, Mr. Williams."

"Williams?"

"As in Tennessee. If we're going to talk gothic, we have to stay in the South."

"Fine by me." Standing in the doorway to the dining room, he smiled at her. "I figured it was time to let some light into my dark and scary castle."

As he spoke, he flipped the wall switch, and the chandelier now dominating the center of the ceiling exploded with light.

She'd been distracted when she arrived, which was the

only rational explanation for not noticing the fixture before. Dozens of candles with crystal tips simulating flames rested on curved pipes finished in burnished copper. The facets of light flickered so realistically, she wouldn't have been surprised to hold her hand toward them and feel heat. The entire room glowed with soft, romantic light.

"Wow," she managed to say.

"It would have been real candles or gas lights back then, of course," Aidan said. "So I commissioned an artist in New Orleans to replicate the effect."

Still staring up, Sloan walked around to look at the chandelier from other angles. "The detail is amazing." It would look fantastic on the historical society brochures.

If Aidan ever let a photographer within fifty feet of it, of course.

"You're impressed," he said, sounding pleased.

"I am. A big-city guy with big-time corporate money buys the most historically significant house on the island, and you wonder whether it's a whim or an investment."

"It's neither to me."

Hearing the anger in his voice, she looked at him instead of the light fixture. "So what is it, Aidan? What brought you here?"

"Penance."

If any man besides Father Dominick had said that word, she probably would have laughed.

But she had no desire to laugh at Aidan. He was deadly serious.

For a moment, she wondered if the ugly, speculative stories about him were true, but her father claimed it was likely Aidan's parents had been killed by a mugger, a drug-addled nut who'd gunned down two people outside a restaurant simply for the cash in their wallets.

Walking toward him, keeping her tone as calm and measured as her steps, she asked, "Penance for what?" He turned his head, but she laid her hand against his cheek and brought him back to face her. "What have you done that you need to make up for?"

"Nothing. It's—" He shook his head, and she was sure if he could he'd have taken back the revealing word. "This house is broken. I want to fix it. That's it."

That wasn't nearly it.

"I needed a new challenge," he added, bringing fuel to her blaze of certainty that whatever had hurt him was in no way simple. "Big-city executives—we need a thrill a minute to survive."

Liar, she thought, though she nodded. "I'll bet. Let's eat. I'm starved."

The relief in his eyes was obvious, but she said nothing about it and led the way to the kitchen. While waiting for the pasta to boil, she caught him up on the latest town gossip, involving a salesman from Chicago who'd come into Courtney's beauty shop last month and, with a disgusting leer, insisted on having the "special hair and massage package." No doubt, Aidan couldn't have cared less about the silly story, but since the spotlight was off him, he seemed more relaxed.

"So, while Courtney's flustered about how to tell the guy to jump in the lake without sounding rude—"

"A special talent among Southern women."

"—Helen—she's our local real-estate agent and happened to be in the shop having her hair highlighted—tells the guy that prostitution, with special massages or otherwise, isn't legal in South Carolina and to get lost."

"Helen is the agent my lawyer dealt with about this house?" Aidan asked.

"Yep."

"I heard a lot about her. 'A tough dame' was my attorney's exact quote."

"Well, this guy hadn't heard about Helen. He had the nerve to wink at her and say 'I hear Realtors around here offer even more exclusive services than the beauty shops.'"

Aidan winced. "So, did she punch the guy?"

"Surprisingly, no. She suggested he find his way to I-75 and the topless cafés."

"And he accepted that?"

"Unfortunately not. But Courtney threatened to call my dad if he didn't move along. So, apparently, the threat of the cops *and* the intimidating factor of a fiery redhead salon owner in steel-tipped cowboy boots *and* an annoyed real-estate agent with her hair sticking out in foil highlight packets was more than he wanted to deal with. He ran out pretty quick."

"A wise move."

Sloan sighed. "If only somebody had been there to record the moment visually. You know, for posterity."

"And the amusement of the townfolk."

"Naturally." She smiled, the picture in her mind giving her a pretty good feeling all on its own. "I haven't laughed so hard since the last time a carload of tourists from Connecticut drove in looking for a tour of the alligator breeding farms."

Aidan's dark eyebrows rose. "You have alligator breeding farms?"

"No way. Down here we have plenty of gators swimming in ponds and crossing roads. Over in Hilton Head they even trot around on the golf courses. Why the hell would we want to make more of them?"

"I see your point." He angled his head. "But do alligators trot?"

"I have no idea." She considered the idea. "Probably not. Bad description—too cute. They probably stalk. Personally, I've never hung around long enough to watch them move more than a step or two."

"Another wise move."

The timer for the pasta buzzed, so Aidan drained the water, while she pulled plates from the cabinets.

"I don't have a dining-room table yet," he said. "It's not coming for a few weeks."

She shrugged. "The kitchen table works for me."

He stared at the battered table shoved into the corner of the kitchen for a long moment. "There was a time I would have had matching candles and place settings, jazz on the stereo." He ran a hand over his stubble-shadowed jaw. "A coat and tie. Everything planned to the tiniest detail."

"And since you don't, I'm leaving."

He shifted his gaze to her, and the wariness she saw made her long to step backward. "Are you?" Aidan asked.

"Leaving?"

He nodded.

Fighting for casualness, she brushed her hand across his chest. "No."

They sat at the battered table, just as they had the night they'd met. Tonight, though, the atmosphere was considerably more relaxed. Maybe there could have been matching candles, fancy place settings and tuxedoed waiters. But she didn't miss them.

As they talked, Sloan saw longer glimpses of the man Aidan must have been before his parents' deaths and whatever had followed had damaged his spirit so thoroughly. Talking about the house and its renovation brought out genuine enthusiasm, and since historical homes were a passion of hers, as well, they had no trouble filling dinner conversation with that topic.

When the doorbell rang, they ignored it.

At least until the door opened, then closed a moment later.

"Anybody home?" Davis called.

Aidan met Sloan's gaze. His eyes were the color of newly honed steel. "I'm buying a lock first thing tomorrow."

She tossed her napkin onto her plate. "Only if you get in line at the hardware store before me."

When Davis appeared in the doorway between the kitchen and the hall, Sloan glared at him.

"Here you are," Davis said, spotting Sloan, then offered a smile that at one time would have turned her insides to pudding.

At the moment, she channeled Helen's ballsy spirit and fought the urge to punch him.

Davis glanced from her to Aidan and back. "I'm not interrupting, am I?"

Her pulse pounding with fury, Sloan rose. "Yes, you are."

"Oh, well, I'm—"

"And you know you are." She grabbed his arm and steered him toward the door that led to the backyard. "Let's talk."

"Okay, if you insist," Davis said, trying to look politely reluctant and failing miserably.

Sloan cast an apologetic glance at Aidan. "This won't take long."

Outside, she released Davis and paced away from him. The warmth of the spring sun had given way to a cool evening, but she didn't feel the temperature drop. Probably because her blood was boiling.

He hadn't charged into Aidan's house when she happened to be there twice in one week by mistake. Was he jealous? Did he really want her back? Was she just convenient and Aidan simply in the way? Or was he here to one-up his former boss for a past conflict that had nothing to do with her at all?

"What are you doing here?" she asked into the thick silence.

"I wanted to see you. I've missed you, Sloan."

She closed her eyes against the warm expression on his face. How many times had she hoped he'd come back and say those words? How many times had she doubted letting him go or wondered if she should have gone after him? Now he'd shown up just as she was getting her life back on track, just as she'd found another man she was interested in.

She forced a glare at him. "So you show up after six months, while I'm on a date?"

"*Date?* I thought you were here to examine his house for the historical society."

"I do that, as well. Tonight, I'm on a date, and you're not welcome."

Sighing, he grasped her shoulders. "Why haven't you returned my calls?"

She shrugged off his touch. "I've been busy."

"Not too busy for Aidan."

Hearing the insult in his voice, she winced. She wasn't trying to hurt him, but she wasn't going to run to his side just because he'd decided to come back home. The betrayal she'd felt when he left still lingered. Who knew how long this whim to visit would last? She simply didn't trust his motives for being on the island or in Aidan's house.

"We'll have lunch next week," she said finally.

"Lunch?" he asked as if she'd invited him to kiss her ass. He cupped her cheek in his hand. "Is that all you want? Can you honestly tell me lunch would satisfy you?"

There'd been a time when Davis had satisfied a great many parts of her. When he'd been the center of her world. But he'd thrown that away. The emotions that went with knowing someone her entire life, someone she thought she'd spend her future with, only to have those dreams shattered by an abrupt exit, vibrated inside her like a volcano on the verge of exploding.

She wasn't ready to invite anything more than lunch. Besides, the crudeness of his question didn't help his case.

"That's all I want from you," she said, meeting his gaze.

His other hand slid around her waist, pulling her against him. The hard, lean planes of his chest were familiar…comforting. "I want a great deal more," he said, dipping his head to kiss her.

There was no way she was kissing one man while on a date with another. She pushed against him. "You need to take a giant step back."

Again, shock flickered across his face. Had she really been such a sap before that he thought a few caresses and flirty words would get her back into his arms?

Even so, she found she wasn't tempted to see if the heat they'd once had still existed. She wanted to see where the chemistry between her and Aidan would lead. She wanted to kiss Aidan, to feel his heart hammering beneath her hands.

Embarrassingly, she wasn't sure she'd be quite so decisive if she hadn't met Aidan. Maybe Davis's confidence and charming smile would have led her exactly where he seemed to want to go.

But she *had* met Aidan. So she was decisive.

"You need to go," she said, turning away. "I have a date to get back to."

AIDAN HEARD the back door open, then close.

Somehow during the last several minutes, he'd managed to clench the stem of his wineglass and sit quietly—if not calmly—at the kitchen table while Sloan and Davis communed in the backyard.

He wanted to toss the other man out on his ass. He wanted to demand Sloan's complete attention.

And why?

Why did it matter if Davis was back in town, and he wanted Sloan? Did it really matter if Sloan wanted him back? Aidan had plenty of his own crap to deal with. He didn't need anybody else's problems. He didn't need anybody else at all.

He never should have agreed to this dinner thing. He was supposed to be exorcising his demons, to be rebuilding his life—board by board, nail by nail. He should be simplifying his life, not complicating it with erotic thoughts and idiotic, jealous impulses.

So when he looked up and saw Sloan standing beside him—and his heart leaped in response—he scowled at her. "Back already?"

She returned to her seat. "I told you it wouldn't take long."

Aidan sipped his wine and pretended serenity. "After six months, I thought you'd have a lot to talk about."

"We'll talk sometime, but not here and not now."

The door opened again, and this time Davis walked into the kitchen. "You're not turning your back on me," he said, his fists clenched at his sides.

"Go home, Davis," Sloan said, not looking up.

"I need to talk to you."

"We'll have lunch," she said, waving her hand vaguely.

"That's not good enough."

Slowly, Aidan rose from his seat. He'd had enough of Davis's lame interruptions and overbearing attitude—and in his house, too. "Sloan has made what she wants perfectly clear."

Davis glared at him. "If you think I'm going to stand aside while you take advantage of a kindhearted, vulnerable lady, you're out of your mind."

"Sloan may be kindhearted, but she can take care of herself."

"So butt out. A lady like Sloan isn't for you."

Aidan was fairly certain that this confrontation had nothing to do with Sloan, and if Davis wanted to make a jerk of himself in front of her, he'd be happy to help out. "Oh, but she is."

Davis puffed out his chest. "No, she isn't."

With an annoyed sigh, Sloan rose and planted herself between Aidan and Davis. "*Hellooo*...standing right here. I'd appreciate if you two would—"

"You need to accept that this is something you can't have," Davis said.

"I had no idea your resentment of me was so personal, Curnan."

"What resentment? What's personal?" Sloan asked, though neither he nor Davis enlightened her.

Davis continued glaring at Aidan. "This has nothing to do with work." He smirked. "Though if you would've just let me do my job, you might not have been forced to sell the company."

"I wasn't forced to sell it."

"That's not what I hear."

Aidan shrugged. He wasn't about to discuss his reasons for selling the company with Davis. How typical of him to think it was all about sales numbers and profits.

"Tell Sloan about your relationship track record," Davis continued to Aidan. "It's not like it's a big secret. Everybody in the company knew about your reputation. Not to mention anybody who watched sensationalized news shows."

Sloan glared at her ex. "Davis!"

The innuendo about him courtesy of the media didn't even phase Aidan, though he appreciated Sloan wasn't the kind of person to believe everything she heard.

Especially when, regarding him anyway, absolutely none of it was true.

Instead, he reminded himself that Davis was a pro at double-talk, at twisting conversations to suit his agenda—yet another reason he hadn't liked his tactics as a sales manager. Clients needed schmoozing from time to time, but they didn't need empty promises and manipulation.

And Davis was really reaching if Aidan's romantic past was all the ammunition he could muster to discourage Sloan from seeing him. His true mistakes were far more damning.

"You seem to be the one dying to tell her." Aidan crossed his arms over his chest. "By all means, please do."

"Sloan, honey," Davis began, sliding his gaze to her, bracing his hands on her shoulders. "Aidan isn't the kind of man you should be with."

"Hmm."

If Davis missed the sarcasm in her voice, Aidan certainly didn't.

"He sees a lot of women," Davis continued. "He doesn't have relationships. He has conquests. When he's gotten what he wants from you, he'll cast you aside."

"Last time I checked, popularity wasn't a crime," Aidan said, wishing he'd resisted offering even that weak defense. Davis was telling the truth—mostly, anyway. Though he didn't much care for the term *conquests*.

Honestly though, he wasn't into serious relationships. The women he dated knew that. He never lied or pretended. Most of the time, they weren't interested in a long-term thing, either. He didn't imagine that he'd left a chain of broken hearts behind in Atlanta.

What he'd had was fun. He liked women, and he had plenty of money and charm to show them a good time.

At least that used to be his life.

Now, those days seemed as if they'd been lived by someone else.

He'd come to Palmer's Island to be alone. To recover and figure out what to do with the rest of his life. To find a way to deal with his grief, anger and frustration. Sloan shouldn't have a role in that recuperation.

Davis was right. She shouldn't be with a man like him.

Sloan narrowed her eyes at Davis. "And I'm such an innocent that I'm ripe for a conquest, huh?"

"You trust people too easily."

"So you're graciously going to let me know the score."

"I care about you, Sloan."

"And yet *you* left me."

"That was—"

"Asinine? Hurtful?"

"A mistake."

Aidan watched their exchange and felt like a dirty voyeur. And in his own house. He didn't come here to meet people, to make friends and *care*. To long for a woman like Sloan and think of her in no way like a conquest. He wanted to touch her lightness, even as he didn't want to infect her with his darkness.

"Why don't you two finish the wine?" he said, heading out of the room. "I'm going back to work."

Sloan caught up to him in the foyer. "You're letting him wreck our date?" she asked, grabbing his arm and dragging him to a stop.

"I'm not letting him do anything. He's right. You shouldn't be with me."

"Ah…so you're being noble."

He was uncomfortable with that description for a great many reasons. "I'm being honest."

"And Davis is being helpful. Gee, with all these big, strong men around taking care of me, I don't need to worry my pretty little head about anything, do I?"

"Your description, not mine. I have no intention of talking to you as though you're four."

"The way Davis was doing?"

"I also have no intention of commenting about Davis. Whatever's between you two needs to be handled without my interference."

"You're not going to fight him for me?"

"No." He stared at her. "Do you want me to?"

"No." She shook her head, disappointment clear in her eyes. "But I'd rather you didn't storm out now. I'd rather you tell him to leave, or at least act like you care about being with me."

He wasn't sure how to answer that challenge. He did care. But he shouldn't.

"He's only here to annoy you," she said. "And maybe win me back. If he's persistent enough, he thinks he'll get his way." She angled her head. "And it's worked, hasn't it?"

"I guess it has."

She threw up her hands. "Super. That's just super." Her face flushed with anger. "I've had enough of men." She stomped into the kitchen, returning with her salad bowl and her purse. "Maybe Sister Mary Katherine can get me a spot in the damn order."

Strangely aroused by her annoyance, Aidan followed her to the door. "You might not want to call it the *damn* order when you apply."

"Yeah, I'll think about that." After she'd opened the door, she glanced at him over her shoulder. "Don't even think about trying to kiss me."

He frowned. "I wasn't thinking about it until you brought it up."

"If you think I'm suffering with sexual frustration alone, think again."

Well, hell. Now he was thinking about a lot more than kissing her. His heart rate zipped into overdrive. Sloan wanted him. Maybe even as much as he wanted her.

"Call me when you're done being noble," she said, giving him a challenging glare. "Otherwise, I'll see you Wednesday."

"Wednesday?"

"For my weekly inspection. If that's convenient for you."

"Yeah. Sure. Whatever."

"Your tendency to gush and make me feel welcome in your home is one of your finest qualities."

"Sloan, I—"

She simply shook her head. Then walked out the door, closing it with a snap behind her.

"That went well," he muttered, pushing his hand through his hair. "You should give lessons in romance, Kendrick. You're a real pro."

"Obviously you've lost your touch."

Aidan turned to face Davis—whom he'd forgotten was even there. "And *you're* still here. This gets better and better."

"I want her back."

"I sort of figured that." Aidan knew he shouldn't want her, but he did. He should be noble, but he wasn't. "I'm not here to use her, then cast her aside."

"Fine. How do we settle this?"

"With whiskey."

5

"AIDAN?"

Only hours later, Sloan peeked around the edge of the front door, and again questioned why she'd come back.

Since the first floor was pitch-black, and she couldn't hear anything except her own annoying thoughts and her own breathing, she still didn't have an answer.

She and Aidan were growing closer. He'd started to relax around her. The connection between them was becoming more than physical. Then the damn ex had to show up, and send him back to his brooding.

And probably the whiskey.

Which was why her conscience had forced her back to his house. In his misery and anger—which she hoped had been brought on by his wild frustration at letting her leave earlier—he might fall down the stairs. Or trip over a sawhorse.

Or he might be sleeping peacefully in his bed.

She debated her intrusion for another ten seconds, then flipped the switch to the tiny flashlight dangling from her key ring. "Aidan? It's Sloan," she called to the silent house as she crept forward. "I just came back to check on you."

Casting her light along the wall, she searched for the table lamp and sawhorse that had been sitting in the corner the first night she arrived.

It was missing.

With a sigh, she swung her flashlight on the opposite side of the foyer, toward the parlor. There was a shadow of something…

She inched toward it, and the closer she got, she realized it was the sawhorse and lamp. "Thank goodness," she said as she flipped the switch. "Aidan, are you—"

As she spoke, she turned, and there, at the base of the steps, was a man's body, facedown in a pool of blood.

Her heart jumped, and she paused for a moment, blinking as her eyes tried to communicate with her brain. As she raced toward him, some part of her registered that the man wasn't Aidan. An orange-and-white baseball cap had been knocked askew, revealing golden-brown hair.

Pete.

There was no way to avoid the blood. There was so much of it. What could he have done to cause such an injury?

"Pete!" She crouched and shook his shoulder, but got no response. Should she turn him? What if he'd injured his spine?

The blood, you idiot. Stop the blood.

She rolled him over. The blood had soaked his shirt and jeans. There were obvious stab wounds in his chest. His eyes were open—and blank.

"Oh, Pete."

Even as her breath caught and sorrow washed over her, she reached into her purse for her cell phone.

What had happened?

Had he surprised an intruder?

Before she could dial, the front door swung open, and the idea that whoever had attacked Pete might have come back zipped through her mind. Her gaze flew to the opening. Where Aidan and Davis stood.

More like swayed.

"Sloan." Aidan smiled slightly. "What are you—" His gaze hit on Pete and the blood. "What the hell…"

He was beside her in an instant, grabbing her arm and pulling her against his chest. "Are you hurt? What happened?"

"I'm fine." Though she felt much better pressed against Aidan's warm body. The vision of Pete's sightless eyes wasn't likely to leave her anytime soon. "It's all Pete's—" her voice caught "—blood."

"What happened?" Aidan repeated.

"I don't know. I just got here and…found him." Suddenly she realized he'd been out somewhere, but what if he'd been here with Pete? What if any of them had come in minutes earlier and interrupted, or become part of, whatever had happened to Pete? "Where were you?"

"Being crazy." Aidan studied her. "Are you sure you're okay?"

The concern in his smoky eyes made her heart race for an entirely different reason than it had been. "Oh, I'm just peachy," she lied.

"Can we sit down, then?" asked Aidan. "I'm not too steady on my feet."

"I'm a little shaky myself," she replied. "What about—" She stopped as she noticed Davis in the front doorway, leaning against the frame, his eyes closed. "Where the devil have you two been?" she demanded.

"Drinking," Aidan said as he sank onto the stairs.

"You were at Velma's?" At his surprised look, she added, "It's the only bar on the island." Avoiding a glance at Pete's body, she sat on the step next to Aidan and flipped open her phone. Her hands were stained with blood, and they shook as she pressed the buttons.

Aidan grimaced. "Who are you calling?"

"My dad."

When her dad picked up, his voice was as strong and commanding as always. "You all right?" he asked, obviously noting her number on the caller ID.

"I'm fine, Daddy." Even on Palmer's Island, the sheriff got enough late-night calls to know it was rarely good news. "I need you to come out to Batherton House. And bring Doc Shepherd."

There was a short pause. "Who's dead?"

"Pete Willis."

"Don't touch anything. I'm on my way."

She didn't see any point in telling him it was too late for that and signed off. She glanced over at Aidan. He looked kind of vulnerable and sweet with his eyes glassy and unfocused. After finding some towelettes in her purse and wiping off her bloodstained fingers, she asked, "How did you get home? Please tell me you didn't drive."

"Some guy at the bar dropped us off."

"Hank. He's the bartender and designated driver. We don't have cabs."

"Could have been him. It's all a bit fuzzy." He dropped his head in his hands. "Finding a dead body in your house is a pretty sobering event, though."

"I'll second that." The adrenaline of the last few minutes was wearing off, replaced by shock. She was cold and desperately wanted a hot shower. Jumping in Aidan's lap was also a good option.

"We should probably move Davis," Sloan said to distract herself from the lure of comfort.

"Why?"

"My dad doesn't like him very much."

Aidan shrugged. "He's all right."

"You guys bonded over whiskey and decided to stop fighting over me?"

"We weren't fighting over you."

"You were drinking over me."

Lifting his head, Aidan stared at her. "Confident, are you?"

"You weren't drinking over me?"

"Maybe."

She rolled her eyes. Aidan didn't seem like the kind of guy to play games. But neither did he seem like the kind of guy to drink himself into a stupor over a woman. Was she special or just a particularly interesting prize? Did either of them care about her at all or only about besting the other? "Are you happy you won?"

"Who says I won?"

"You're the conscious one."

"Right." He stood. "I'm going to make coffee."

Trying not to take his avoidance personally, she rose, as well. "We have to stay put until my dad gets here. We can't touch anything."

"I can't sit here and pretend Pete isn't dead!"

The explosion of anger didn't surprise her. And though she understood his frustration and sense of unease, she'd been part of law enforcement all her life and understood the necessity of staying calm and controlled. Anger wouldn't bring Pete back. And tears would, no doubt, come later.

She joined her hand with Aidan's. "Let's wait on the porch."

"Fine." He pulled away and stalked out the door, snagging Davis by the arm as he went. Davis snorted awake, then stumbled alongside his former boss.

"Wha…wha…happened?"

"There's a tornado coming, so we're taking shelter under the palms," Sloan said.

Davis squinted, then shrugged. "Sure. Okay."

"What did you give him?" Sloan asked Aidan as they helped Davis to sit, then propped him against the porch's railing.

Aidan looked annoyed. "*I* didn't give him anything. He ordered from the bartender."

"You ordered whiskey, and he copied you."

"How am I supposed to be responsible for—"

"Davis isn't much of a drinker." She paused, glancing at her former lover, slumped and snoozing openmouthed a few feet away. "Coffee maybe, but certainly not whiskey."

Aidan smirked, as if holding your own against a bottle of Jack Daniels was some kind of test of manhood.

Which, basically, where she lived, was true.

"How'd you two ever get together anyway?" Aidan asked.

She looked at her potential lover, who, while bleary-eyed, was still pretty steady on his feet. She was comparing the two men to distract herself from Pete and from the familiar horror she and Aidan had yet to get through that night.

The coroner and the cops.

The mechanical procedure of examining and moving the body was all the more disturbing for its quiet routine. Though her father had tried to protect her, she'd still managed to get involved in things she shouldn't many times in the past. She knew about the whispered supposition and probing questions that would follow.

And there was no way the next few hours wouldn't bring back memories for Aidan.

His parents' deaths three months ago. And because of the Kendrick name, the story had been thrust into the spotlight, then later complicated by Aidan's lack of patience and cooperation with the reporters.

Now, in light of Pete's death, new questions about Aidan's past were racing through her mind.

Had Aidan been there with his parents? Was it a simple mugging or not? Did he blame himself? Was that why he needed penitence?

She was happy to distract him—and herself. "High school," she answered to his question about meeting Davis.

"Let me guess—you were the head cheerleader, and he was the star quarterback."

"I *was* the head cheerleader, as a matter of fact, but he was the nerdy kid with glasses and a pocket protector. And we actually didn't start dating until years after graduation. By then, I was falling for the smart, vulnerable ones."

"He always seemed sure of himself to me."

She rested against the house, facing Aidan and realizing she still went for the smart, vulnerable ones. "The confidence came later. The arrogance was really recent."

"About the time he was stupid enough to leave you?"

Beneath the dim porch light, she watched the turbulent emotions swimming in his eyes. Not all of them were for her of course, but some were. He wanted her, but didn't think he should have her? What was that about? What had they fallen into? How could this fledgling attraction survive a troubling past, an intruding ex and a murder?

She had no idea, but she wanted it to.

"Yes," she said finally. "About then."

Headlights cut through the night, interrupting anything Aidan might have wanted to say.

Sloan turned away from him and watched the headlights of her father's pickup break through the overgrown shrubs crowding the driveway. Seconds later, the big black diesel truck stopped in front of the house. The sheriff dropped out of the driver's side, straightened his six-foot-six frame, then sauntered toward the porch, his pistol holstered at his side.

She walked toward him, meeting him on the sidewalk. He hugged her tight against his broad chest. "What're you doing here, little girl, covered in blood and messin' up my crime scene?"

She glanced down at her shirt, smeared with Pete's dried blood. She shifted her gaze to her father, ridiculously grateful to have him take over. "I didn't know that it was a crime scene then, Daddy."

"Uh-huh. You oughta know what a dead body looks like by now, as many times as you come meddlin' into my cases."

"It's the twenty-first century, Daddy. Women don't meddle. Besides, it was dark. I was startled."

"You seem pretty calm now."

"Somebody had to take charge."

"That's my girl. Where's your gun?"

"In the glove box of my car."

He frowned.

"This is Palmer's Island, Daddy. Do you really think I need to carry my gun at all times?"

"A good question to ask Pete. If we could."

She'd been raised by a strong, hard lawman. Her mother had died of cancer before her second birthday. She was used to abrupt conversation and no conversation. Burying her emotions and doing what needed to be done was as common as breathing.

Underneath, though, she knew she was his princess. She knew tears from a child reduced him to a complete puddle. She knew a stray dog in his town always found a home.

She knew Pete's unexpected, violent death angered and

insulted him. He took the safety of his citizens very seriously, and he'd work until he dropped to make sure justice was served.

No matter how many times in the past she'd helped him with cases—though he might refer to that as *interference*—she was a freakin' librarian. This wasn't her forte.

"Can you take over now, so I can collapse and cry in the corner?"

His hands, so large, comforting and familiar, massaged her shoulders. "It's bad?"

Her mind flashed back to her first look at Pete. She swallowed. "Yes."

He glanced behind her. "That the Kendrick boy?"

"He's hardly a boy, Daddy."

His sandy-silver eyebrows arched. "Yeah?"

"Don't make trouble."

"Whoever spilled Pete's blood made the trouble."

"You know what I mean. Don't try to intimidate Aidan."

"Oh, it's Aidan, is it?"

She noticed he didn't make any promises regarding intimidation. Her dad's deep-South accent and slow speech rhythm had fooled many into underestimating his cleverness.

"We're dating," she clarified. Though were they? She'd never really gotten an answer from Aidan to whether she was the prize in his and Davis's Neanderthal drinking game. "Sort of."

"Then what's that big-city dummy doing sleeping on the porch?"

Daddy's eyesight was also pretty keen. "Davis and Aidan were at Velma's earlier."

"Boy never could hold his liquor."

Sloan rolled her eyes. How she'd become a successful, modern woman surrounded by people with ancient-history mentalities, she'd never know. But now was as good a moment as any to run through the timeline. "Aidan and I had dinner earlier. Davis interrupted, so I left. Aidan and Davis went drinking at Velma's. I came back here, looking for Aidan, found Pete instead. Aidan and Davis showed up just after, then I called you."

Her dad mulled over the explanation for a few seconds. "There are a lot of details in there you left out."

"But none that have anything to do with the murder." She glanced back at Aidan, still standing on the porch. A first date that ended in homicide? Not a promising beginning to a relationship. She slid her hand into her dad's. "Let's get this over with."

AIDAN, though he stood on the porch, didn't have to look down to meet the sheriff's bright-blue gaze.

The eye color was the only thing that he'd passed on to his daughter, as the rest of him was tall, broad and hardened like steel. He wore a brown Stetson, which added to his height, and even though it was past midnight, his jeans and shirt looked pressed by patient hands. He also looked as if he'd just walked off the set of an Old West movie.

"Don't let my size fool ya, boy," he said slowly in a thick Southern accent. "I can also shoot the eye off a rattlesnake at fifty feet."

He grinned, though even that seemed to be a threat.

"Stop it," Sloan said, nudging her father.

"Stop what?"

"Intimidating."

The sheriff's brows came together as he looked down at his daughter, so tiny next to him, she resembled a fairy. A really annoyed fairy.

"I'm just standing here," he said defensively.

"I haven't even introduced you, and you're already talking about your gun."

"He was lookin' at me."

"You make a dramatic first impression, if you recall."

The sheriff drew back his shoulders. "I do, don't I?"

"Daddy…"

Aidan liked watching them. Well, looking at Sloan was never a hardship. But concentrating on them helped him forget his nausea and the despair that threatened to crush him. Too many memories, too much whiskey and the sight of blood on his recently-polished wooden floor were not a good combination.

"Fine then." The sheriff closed the distance between him and Aidan and held out his hand—roughly the size of a bus. "Sheriff Buddy Caldwell. You must be our new resident, Aidan Kendrick."

"Yes, sir, Sheriff."

"You get moved in okay? People making you feel welcome?"

"Yes, sir."

"Good, good. I expect you'll have quite a few more callers after this nasty business tonight."

Great. All he wanted was to be left alone—with the exception of Sloan—and his house had more traffic than the bar.

"You mess with my little girl, and I'll run you out of town before you can blink."

"Daddy!"

Aidan simply held her father's gaze and nodded. "Yes, sir."

Davis mumbled in his sleep, and everybody turned toward him.

"We can't just leave him here," Sloan said.

"Sure we can." The sheriff's eyes narrowed as he glanced back at Aidan. "You match him, drink for drink?"

"I did."

He clapped Aidan on the shoulder, and they headed into the house. "Call me Buddy."

The casual friendliness disappeared the moment the three of them stood in the foyer. Pete's body lay still near the base of the stairs. A graphic reminder that they hadn't gathered for a social purpose.

"Should I get a sheet to cover him?" Aidan asked, his stomach clenching.

"No," Sloan and the sheriff said together.

"We can't contaminate the crime scene," Sloan added.

Even as Aidan wondered what Sloan knew about crime scene procedures, her father walked toward the body and stared down for a moment or two. "Looks like he was stabbed." He crouched. "There are five, maybe six wounds."

"What was he doing here?" Sloan asked, turning toward Aidan. "He left earlier for a hot date. Why come back?"

The shock of finding Pete, and knowing *Sloan* had found Pete, was becoming reality. The memories of seeing his parents' die and his guilt over that weighed just as heavily.

Why was this happening in his house?

Why was he in the middle—again—of sorrow and violence?

He'd tried to escape his past by coming to sleepy Palmer's Island. Instead, he was back where he started.

"Maybe he returned for something," he managed to suggest.

"At midnight?"

"He knows I stay up late."

"Who hated him so much?" Sloan asked.

"What makes you think somebody hated him?" her father asked.

"He's dead. Violently dead."

With concentrated effort, Aidan blinked away memories. "Not all violence is about hatred," he said quietly.

He could feel Sloan's and the sheriff's stares and knew he was handling the situation badly. He wanted to be strong for her, yet he was positive he was the only one who wanted to run from the room, to abandon Pete and all his death represented.

"Why don't you make us some coffee, Sloan?" the sheriff said. "I expect Doc will want some when he gets here."

Sloan's gaze slid to Aidan. "Well, I—"

"I'll make coffee," he said, turning away.

The sick dread in his stomach eased somewhat as he walked down the hall. But guilt returned with a vengeance.

What kind of man was he to leave Sloan with that scene while he hid?

The mechanics of putting coffee into the filter and filling the pot with water should have made him feel more normal. Instead, it only exacerbated his feelings and the surrealistic nature of everything going on around him. Why was he making coffee when Pete, the easygoing, talented carpenter, was gone?

As he heard footsteps behind him, he paused and tensed.

"It's only me," Sloan said. "I asked my dad to give us a few minutes alone." She paused, then, "This brings back memories of your parents."

It wasn't a question, and he said nothing.

She linked her hand with his. "You found them, didn't you? The night they died?"

He closed his eyes against the sympathy and understanding in her voice. "Not now. I can't do this now."

"It's all pretty intense." She squeezed his hand. "Some date."

"Yeah, I guess so."

"Wanna do it again?"

His eyes flew open. Looking at her, at the hope and—crazy as it was—*humor* in her eyes, the tightness within him eased a bit. Being with her seemed the only right thing in his life, yet he still hesitated. Dragging her into his darkness wasn't fair.

As the sound of other voices drifted in from the foyer, she let go of his hand and stepped back. "That'll be Doc Sheppard…the coroner."

"Would you mind waiting for the coffee to finish?" he asked. "I should go out there. It's my house."

She held his gaze. "You don't have to."

"Yes, I do."

Though his feet felt like lead, he walked down the hall toward the front door. He greeted the coroner, the representative from the funeral home and a photographer from the local paper, who doubled as the crime-scene documenter. He answered the sheriff's questions about the work Pete had been doing for him and tried to provide any details he could remember about the carpenter's personal life.

Unfortunately, he knew little beyond the fact that Pete had excellent woodworking skills and always seemed to have a date. Aidan had been so wrapped up in his own life and issues, he'd not taken a lot of notice of others'.

That would have to change, he realized, as the sheriff and the coroner went about their jobs. As Sloan walked into the foyer with cups of steaming hot coffee on a tray. As whispered speculation became theories, which only led to more questions and speculation. Pete's death was his responsibility now.

Maybe he could actually do right by somebody this time.

Eventually, the body was loaded onto a stretcher and wheeled out the door in a black bag on a gurney. The doctor and his people followed, then the sheriff shook his hand and walked outside.

The sheriff exchanged a long glance with his daughter as she stood on the porch.

"I'll be right there," Sloan said quietly, then she turned toward Aidan, her eyes bright with interest. "Wanna do it again?"

After all they'd been through that night, she wanted to talk about dates. Either she was a great deal stronger than him, she was really interested in him or she was beyond reasonably optimistic. Were all three even possible?

"You're serious?" he said, cramming his hands in the front pockets of his jeans. "Our first date was interrupted by your ex and ended with my carpenter's murder. You really want to get together again?"

She stepped close and laid her hands on his chest. The tropical scent of her perfume, the allure of her body and the pleasure and escape she could bring washed over him, somehow blocking out everything else that had happened.

"Definitely," she whispered just before she covered his mouth with hers.

The fact that her father—her huge, easily annoyed, overly protective father—stood several feet away only passed through his consciousness for a moment. The rest of Aidan accepted her offering with wild gratefulness.

He slid his hands into her hair, cupping her head and angling her face as his tongue moved past her lips, tangling with hers. He delved into her mouth as if he could draw her essence into his. His heart pounded; his blood sang.

Her hands clutched his shirt as their bodies molded together. As her hips bumped his erection, he groaned and slid his hand down her back, pulling her tighter against him. He wanted to devour her, to bury himself inside her so that pain and death didn't have room to exist.

In her, he could escape.

When she pulled back seconds later, her eyes were bright, her breathing labored. Smiling, she ran her thumb across his bottom lip. "Not such a bad end to a date, after all."

Then she turned and strutted away, sexy hips swaying as she moved.

He watched the taillights of her car and her father's truck disappear through the bushes along the driveway and remained standing there for several minutes afterward. He was aroused, saddened, confused and angry.

But knowing he could do nothing about any of those things until at least after sunrise—which, by the look of the sky, wasn't too far off—he headed back inside, avoiding glancing at the spot where Pete's lifeless body had lain.

It was only when he was lying in his bed, staring at the ceiling, wondering what Sloan was doing at that moment, that he remembered Davis was passed out on the porch.

"Well, hell," he muttered, throwing back the covers.

6

AFTER SHAKING Davis awake at nine the next morning, Aidan ignored his rival's complaints about the comfort of the sofa, shoved a disposable cup of coffee in his hand then urged him out the door.

Finally, he was alone.

Despite the tumultuousness of the night before, and wondering about where his relationship with Sloan could really lead in the middle of such chaos, he'd slept hard and woken with a strong sense of purpose.

He had to find Pete's killer.

He'd done little for his parents. Instead of dodging the media, he should have used them. But he'd been too angry at himself and the world to do anything proactive.

Though the Atlanta detective in charge of their case promised he wouldn't forget them, hope had dwindled every day. These things were solved immediately or not at all, he'd been told many times.

Which meant he and Pete didn't have much time.

After working through the morning and into the early afternoon on cleaning the hallway and sanding the stairwell, hoping inspiration would hit him, it suddenly did. Walking into the parlor, he discovered several of the carpenter's tools, including his circular saw, cordless drill, planer and nail gun.

Maybe Pete had come back for one of them.

Though he'd made that suggestion last night and Sloan had discounted it, he knew that Pete was a night owl like him. He'd told Aidan he often worked until two or three in the morning if a solution to a project or a particularly creative idea occurred to him. He could easily have found the door open and decided to help himself to the tools.

But then what?

A crazed maniac had been in the house, stealing Aidan's two-by-fours and whiskey and decided he had to get rid of Pete?

They'd found no weapon and none of the knives in the kitchen were missing. It seemed as though the murderer had brought his weapon with him, so that ruled out impulse. Yet how could he have known Pete would be in Aidan's house at midnight? Had Pete been followed?

And who'd want Pete dead anyway? He was a young, popular and talented carpenter. Somebody not best pleased with their new kitchen cabinets had decided to kill him?

Each scenario seemed as unlikely as the next.

The whole thing—

Ding-dong.

Frowning, Aidan left the parlor and headed to the front door. Who could that be? He glanced at his watch, noting it was just after three. Way too early for Sloan and their dinner date. Did the sheriff have more questions?

He opened the door to find a pair of women standing on his porch, holding what looked like casserole dishes. "You've got the wrong—"

"Aidan Kendrick?" the brunette on the right asked.

He'd never seen these women in his life. Fiftyish, attractive, well-dressed, but he had no idea who they were. "Yeah, but—"

"We've got the right house. I'm Betsy Johnson. This is my friend, Patsy Smith."

"Okay, but—"

"We've come to offer our condolences."

They knew about Pete already? Sloan was right. The only thing that moved fast on this island was gossip. "Don't you usually offer condolences to the family?"

"Oh, Pete didn't have any family in town," the blonde, Patsy, said matter-of-factly. "Can we come in? These dishes are heavy."

"Sure." Still confused, but not seeing how he could turn them away, Aidan stepped back and opened the door wider.

"Where's the kitchen?" Betsy asked, her gaze darting around the foyer.

"We'd love a tour," Patsy said. "I haven't been in this house in nearly twenty years. You're making a lot of improvements, I hear."

Noting that both of their gazes lingered on the bare spot at the base of the stairs, Aidan decided the sheriff or the coroner, or both, were unfamiliar with the word *discreet.* "I am doing extensive renovations," he said, "but I'm really not prepared for tours just yet. Maybe in a few months I'll—"

Ding-dong.

He walked back to the door. This time there was a teenager and a nun—habit and all—standing on the porch. They, too, held casserole dishes.

"We're so sorry to hear about that awful business last night, Mr. Kendrick," the nun said, her brown eyes bright with understanding. She extended her dish, covered with aluminum foil. "We wanted to offer our sympathies."

He took the dish and stepped back to allow them inside. "Uh, thanks."

"I'm Sister Mary Katherine and this is Penelope Waters."

He shook their hands briefly. "Aidan Kendrick."

"Yes, we know." The sister glanced at the teenager—the girl who wasn't supposed to come near him, Aidan recalled from his and Sloan's first meeting. "We're both on the historical committee with Sloan."

Betsy walked toward the nun. "Sister, isn't it just horrible about Pete?"

"Penelope and I were just at the church lighting a candle for his spirit," Sister Mary Katherine returned. "We can take comfort in knowing his soul is at rest."

Patsy shook her head. "Madam Arlene, the psychic next to Courtney's salon, says that a murdered person never rests until his killer is punished."

Betsy sighed. "Honestly. You should know better than to listen to a kook like Arlene."

"She's not a kook," Patsy insisted. "She's very intuitive."

While the two women argued and Sister Mary Katherine soothed, Penelope crossed to the staircase, and since she didn't pause where Pete's body had lain, Aidan assumed at least the adults had had enough sense not to give the lurid details of the murder to a young girl.

"It's lovely," she said, running her hand along the new railing. "Thanks."

She was exactly as he'd pictured—mousy brown hair, big brown eyes wide behind her glasses. "Ms. Caldwell says you're doing an amazing job with the restorations."

"I'm trying. I hear you're pretty skilled with computers. I need to buy one. Maybe you could give me some advice?"

Her eyes, if possible, widened even more. "You don't own a computer?"

"I did. Well, I still have one at my condo in Atlanta. I was thinking of getting a laptop, though."

"What will you use it for?"

"Internet mostly. I need to search sites for antiques and estate sales."

"How much do you want to spend?"

"Whatever it takes for speed."

"Okay, well you'll definitely want to invest in a T1 connection…" She went on to explain the brands she thought were the most reliable and how much memory she thought he'd need.

"Mr. Kendrick, which way to the kitchen?"

Aidan turned to find Patsy, Betsy and the good sister all staring suspiciously at him. "Down the hall," he said, pointing.

"Why don't you show us?" Betsy said, her gaze sliding toward Penelope.

What did they think he was going to do that was so inappropriate around a sixteen-year-old girl? They were the ones who'd brought her to a murder scene. "Yeah, sure."

With little enthusiasm—somehow he didn't think there was a two-inch sirloin in any of those casserole dishes—he led the ladies into the kitchen.

As Betsy and Patsy busied themselves by putting the casseroles in the fridge and expressing their shock over his lack of provisions, Sister Mary Katherine steered him toward the coffeepot. "You have to forgive Betsy and Patsy," she said quietly. "Everyone in the parish is protective of our sweet Penelope."

"You think I'd hurt her?"

"Of course not."

He set about making coffee as he overheard the other women discussing the coffee cake one of them had apparently brought. All he wanted was to be alone. Instead, he was entertaining church women, clearly intent on checking out him and the notorious scene his house had now become.

Last time it had been news reporters with microphones

shoved in his face. Was it better or worse that infamy came in a softer package the second time around?

"She's all alone in the world, so we naturally overreact."

"Who's all alone?" And how could he join them?

"Penelope. She was orphaned at five when her parents were killed in a car accident. The sisters and I took her in and raised her—along with the generosity of church members like Patsy and Betsy. She's a community child." She glanced at Penelope and pride glowed in her eyes. "We think we've done quite well, actually."

Aidan longed to pound his head on the counter. He didn't want to know this stuff. He didn't want to care about these people. He didn't want to picture the smart, innocent and vulnerable Penelope as an orphan.

Like you.

Not like him. Not *at all* like him. He was a grown man and hardly needed church ladies and nuns to take care of him.

"Good grief, Mr. Kendrick," Betsy said in horror. "When was the last time you had a decent meal? You simply can't exist this way."

What was wrong with ham and cheese? He liked ham and cheese.

And he'd put away the damn whiskey—though only because his head had been pounding when he'd woken up and didn't want to look at the bottle. "Look, I—"

"This spaghetti sauce smells pretty good," Patsy said, lifting the top off the stock pot Aidan had put in the fridge after last night's disastrous ending to his date with Sloan.

He'd had about enough of unwanted visitors. He didn't need them snooping through his fridge, their judgment of his lifestyle, and he sure as hell didn't want to answer questions about Pete, which was bound to happen over coffee and cake.

Crossing his arms over his chest, he gave Patsy his fiercest stare. "Pretty good?"

"Oh, my." Betsy's hand fluttered to her chest. "Sloan was certainly right about him, wasn't she?"

"I think we should have cake," Penelope suggested abruptly before Aidan could ask her what Sloan had said about him.

So they sat and had cake at his battered kitchen table while he stood by the counter and felt guilty for not having a more elegant place for them to gather. He also looked quite ragged, dressed in a worn gray T-shirt and faded jeans.

At Penelope's urging, they discussed the renovations and the history of the house. And because the Community Child was present, and he realized he was safe from inquiries into the details of last night, he found himself relaxing a bit. The house was at least a subject he could talk about with some authority and without embarrassment or getting personal.

When the doorbell rang again some minutes later, he breathed a resigned sigh, prepared to welcome the next round of casseroles and wondering if he had enough coffee to serve every church lady in town.

As he opened the door, he plastered on a pleasant smile, which froze, then broadened the moment he saw Sloan.

She extended a big basket, which he took. "How are you holding up?"

She wore dark jeans and a fluttery yellow top that left her shoulders bare, and he barely resisted the urge to fall at her feet in gratitude, appreciation and lust. "I'm not lonely."

"I figured. Put that basket in the library. It's for you, not the church."

Glancing at the contents, he noted chips, cookies and a small bottle of premium whiskey.

"And don't even think about not sharing."

"Am I sharing with you?"

She planted her hands on her hips, her lips tipped up on the sides in a now familiar, but still heart-pounding way. "Who else?"

"Nobody." He led the way to the library, where he set the basket down, then closed the door. "*Do* something. I don't think they're going to leave."

She patted his cheek, and even that simple touch set his skin ablaze. "Poor Aidan. Having a hard time brooding?"

"Yes."

"Patsy, Betsy and Sister Mary Katherine?"

"Yes. How did you—"

"I recognize the cars. Did they bring Penelope?"

He barely resisted groaning. "Yes."

"And told you about how she's being raised?"

"Definitely."

"They're sneaky."

"Why are they here?"

"To comfort you."

"And see where Pete was killed."

Sloan shrugged. "There's an element of morbid curiosity, but mostly they're here because they're worried about you. They don't want you to be alone and grieving."

He stiffened. He wasn't going into his pain over his parents. "I'm sorry for Pete, but I don't need casseroles and coffee cake. I wasn't his family or that good a friend. We'd only just met."

"Yet you grieve."

He clenched his fists. "Don't."

She moved toward him. She slid the back of her hand across his stubble-covered cheek. "Don't what? Don't touch you?" Moving into him, her breasts brushed his chest. "Don't get too close?"

His heart skipped a beat. "There's a nun down the hall."

"Mmm…" She nudged the side of his neck with her nose. "Worried we'll get caught and punished?"

I'm worried I'll care.

But part of him already knew it was too late, part of him knew his chemistry with Sloan was something much deeper. He was powerless to stop it, and weak enough to need it. He could barely breathe when she was around, and all he wanted to do was absorb more of her into him.

He braced his hands on either side of her waist. "Sloan, I…" He trailed off as her lips moved up his jaw.

"Need me? Want me?"

"Yes."

"It's too late to resist."

Yes. Heaven was being offered, and he had a houseful of people he didn't want to know, but already cared about.

He found her lips, the comfort and thrill they offered. He felt alive again when he was with her. He wanted so much of her, yet he was certain he didn't deserve any of this.

"There's a nun down the hall," he reminded her again, even as he moved his mouth down her throat.

Her arms wrapped around his neck, she let her head drop back, so he could kiss his way along her collarbone, then dip between her breasts. "This party is for two only."

He smiled against her skin. Then, picturing the diminutive nun standing by, watching them with censure in her eyes, he laughed. Stopping, he looked down at Sloan. "My life gets more warped by the second. Why am I laughing?"

Sloan seemed slightly annoyed. "I have no idea."

He stroked his fingers across her cheek. "Help me get rid of these people, and you can make me laugh some more."

"You're feeding me, too?"

He winced. "I have leftover spaghetti, and ham and cheese."

"And a lot of casseroles."

"Oh, right." Though he wasn't much for tuna and cream of mushroom soup, which was his experience with casseroles.

"Aren't you lucky that Betsy makes a great chicken casserole, and I brought green beans and homemade bread?"

Though that sounded great, he felt compelled to scowl. "I can feed myself, you know."

"Face it. Without ten restaurants that deliver on speed dial, you're lost."

"I made spaghetti sauce."

"Spaghetti sauce being an exception." She fluffed her hair, then hooked her arm around his. "Well, if we're not going to make out, let's gossip."

"No gossip," he said as he opened the door. "Exits. Lots of exits."

She paused. "You're telling me you don't want to know what happened to Pete and why?" When he said nothing, she added, "You don't feel responsible in some way?"

"Why would I feel responsible?"

She shrugged, though she watched him closely. "Your carpenter. Your house."

"Well, I don't."

"Feel responsible, or want to know what happened?"

Since both of those were true, but he didn't want Miss Intuitive to get all cocky on him, he extended his hand toward the hallway. "Gossip it is."

"I'll give you a two-minute escape if you get the food from my car. Then we'll meet in the kitchen." She turned away. "Don't even think about ditching me."

"Wouldn't dream of it," he said, an honest response since

the memory of that kiss, and the anticipation of more like it, was enough to keep him momentarily content.

When he walked into the kitchen with the box containing Sloan's dishes and a grocery bag of peppers and onions that he assumed fitted into the dinner plans, the ladies' conversation ceased. Their gazes all darted to him, so he was certain he'd been the topic of the discussion.

"Have some cake," Sloan offered, exchanging her plate with the stuff he'd brought from her car.

He realized the pall of death had lightened a bit, since Sloan and the other ladies had arrived. He'd been telling himself for months that he didn't need anyone, that he was better off alone.

He'd been wrong.

While he ate the piece of cake, which was loaded with cinnamon and caramel, he listened to the women talk about upcoming events—the oyster roast being held next weekend, the Memorial Day picnic next month.

Aidan had forgotten what a sense of community was like. When he was younger, living with his parents in the Atlanta suburbs, his neighborhood was always having cookouts and block parties. He was as comfortable in his neighbor's house as he was in his own. The only time he saw his neighbors now in his condo building was in the elevator or parking garage.

His parents had been his last connection to those carefree days. Before board meetings and strategy sessions, before concerns over maximizing profits and minimizing expenses, before empty dates and nights at the clubs.

Now he was truly alone.

"Has anyone heard about a service for Pete?" Sloan asked suddenly, seeming the only one bold enough to mention the reason they'd all gathered in the first place.

Patsy glanced briefly at Penelope, then cleared her throat. "Doc Sheppard said he wasn't sure there would be one. His family—they're in California—were too upset to discuss the…arrangements."

"It'll be a few days anyway," Betsy added. "He's been, uh…moved to the county crime lab."

"For the autopsy," Penelope said, then she casually took a sip of coffee.

The adults all immediately looked uncomfortable.

To his surprise, Sloan turned to him. "Aidan, why don't you give Penelope a tour of the house?"

"I—" Realizing he was being called into community service, he set his plate on the counter. "I'd be glad to."

"I know Pete died," Penelope said matter-of-factly. "Somebody stabbed him. We need to find out who."

"The sheriff will find out who," Sister Mary Katherine said in her serene tone of authority as she rose from her chair. "Penelope and I need to visit Mrs. Brinkley. She had surgery on her bunions yesterday."

Penelope's eyes widened. "But, Sister, I want to help."

"Mrs. Brinkley needs your help just now."

Though she hesitated, Penelope stood, rinsed her own and the nun's dishes in the sink. "I know, Sister."

As the sister exchanged goodbyes with the other women, Aidan saw Penelope catching Sloan's eye and mouthing "Call me."

As soon as they all heard the front door shut, Patsy urged Sloan and Aidan into the vacant chairs, then leaned forward. "So, here's what's really going on at the funeral home…"

Betsy frowned. "We should have respect for Pete."

"I have plenty of respect," Patsy said with a decisive nod. "We have to find his killer, and Sloan is our best shot."

Sloan? Aidan wondered. Hot, sexy, librarian Sloan was going to find Pete's killer? "Isn't that the sheriff's job?"

"Sort of," Betsy said. "But Sloan is the island's own Nancy Drew."

There was a long pause.

"I helped catch a burglar when I was fifteen," Sloan said, her face flushing. "It's one of those kid things you have to constantly live down."

"Sounds pretty ambitious to me." Aidan grinned. "At fifteen I was focused on baseball, girls and—" he glanced at the other ladies "—making sure those girls got home on time to meet their curfew."

"Quick thinkin', Kendrick," Betsy said with a wink. "The sheriff will appreciate that."

"So Pete's body was transferred to the county crime lab this morning," Patsy began. "The autopsy is being scheduled ASAP, mostly because the sheriff made a personal appeal to the forensic people."

Sloan cocked her head. "How do you know what my dad's doing, when I don't know what he's doing?"

"I'm nosier than you," Patsy said with a wave of her hand. "Anyway, the sheriff is extremely concerned. Public safety is an issue."

"Public safety?" Aidan asked with a raised brow. "I don't even have a lock on my front door."

Sloan gave him a big grin, and he had the feeling she'd made a trip to the hardware store, as well as the grocery store since last night. At least they could ignore anybody who wanted to interrupt their dinner.

"Exactly," Patsy said. "When the *Palmer's Island Herald* gets hold of this, you can bet they're going to suggest everyone lock their doors until this maniac is caught."

"Good thing the paper only comes out every two weeks," Sloan said drily.

"I wouldn't be surprised if they printed a special edition," Patsy said. "This whole thing *is* a bit creepy."

Betsy sipped her coffee. "Who says the killer's a maniac? Maybe he's one of us—a regular, law-abiding citizen?"

Patsy shook her head. "What regular, law-abiding citizen would want to kill Pete? He was well liked, easygoing and did extremely good work. He built a deck for Bill and me last summer, and the thing is a work of art. If I sent a picture to *Southern Living,* they'd put it in their magazine in a second."

"I tend to agree with Patsy," Sloan said, shifting in her chair. "We all know everybody in town. Who could have done this? Pete was violently stabbed. Why? Who could have been so angry with him? Instinctively, I favor the idea that a burglar wanted to lift some valuables from the house, and Pete surprised him."

"But the killer brought the weapon, didn't he?" asked Patsy.

"That's true," Sloan said, considering. "And a knife is a pretty personal weapon. A professional burglar would likely go with something distant and nonlethal, like Mace."

Betsy pursed her lips. "We keep saying he. I know that's just a general thing, but what about the idea of a woman? Pete did date a lot. Maybe somebody didn't like being one of the crowd."

"So, who was he dating?" Sloan asked.

Betsy's eyes lit. "Oooh! Like suspects?" She glanced at the others, who all continued to look respectfully sober. "I'm trying to help."

"Of course you are." Sloan reached across the table and patted her arm. "Who was Pete dating?"

Betsy glanced at Patsy before she spoke. "There's Briana, who works the reception desk at Courtney's salon on weekends."

"And Ramona at the diner," Patsy chimed in.

Betsy nodded. "And Karen, the manager of the dry cleaners."

"Oh, don't forget Gretchen."

"Doesn't she teach at the high school?" Betsy asked.

"Yeah. Biology." Patsy frowned. "Or maybe chemistry."

Clearly, unassuming Pete was a major player on Palmer's Island. Or anywhere else for that matter. Even on his most social days, Aidan hadn't gone out with that many women at once—and he'd lived in a city of several million people.

"You've been pretty quiet, Aidan," Sloan said, her gaze meeting his. "What do you think?"

He was thinking he should be disturbed by the conversation, by the fact that Pete had met a violent end like his parents and was now reduced to a topic of gossip and juicy conversation. Like his parents.

Yet beneath the very human tendency toward excitement that mysteries and murder always seemed to induce, he found himself wishing he'd gotten his friends together for a round-table discussion after losing his family. If he'd shared more of his feelings, if he'd talked instead of retreating, could he have helped? Would their killer still be at large?

"I can't imagine anyone wanting to hurt Pete," he said finally. "But love—and the lack of it—makes people do strange things."

"Here, here," Patsy said, raising her coffee cup.

They kicked around more theories and even wild speculation involving Pete having a secret gambling problem and owing money to knee-breaking collectors, but since that type of discussion hit too close to home for Aidan—a fact which Sloan quickly realized—she pushed the discussion around to more sound ideas.

They also realized the sheriff and the forensic people had

plenty of work to do before they would have concrete evidence to go on.

After Patsy and Betsy left, he and Sloan walked back into the kitchen where she started removing things from the grocery bag—peppers, onions, limes, meat wrapped in butcher's paper, a new doorknob and lock kit and a bottle of clear liquor. An odd combination for most dates, but it made sense for them.

"We can install the lock later," she said. "Food and drink first."

He picked up the bottle. "Tequila. We're having chicken casserole and tequila?"

"No, we're having tacos and tequila. I'm saving the casseroles for you for when I'm not around." She slid several limes down the counter. "Start squeezing. We're going to make a kick-ass drink, we'll send out a toast to Pete, we're going to eat, then we're going to dance slow and close, forgetting all about the last, lousy twenty-four hours."

He loved how she meticulously planned everything. "Not all of yesterday was lousy. I distinctly remember some seriously hot kissing."

"We'll do more of that."

"Excellent." He cut the limes then began squeezing them into the shaker Sloan handed him. "So what's in this drink?"

"Lime juice, tequila and a splash of soda water. Sister Mary Katherine would definitely not approve." She glanced at him as he picked up the tequila bottle. "And don't be stingy with that."

"You can count on me."

As he made the drinks, she chopped peppers, onions and steak. With everything sizzling in the pan, he handed her the cocktail and toasted her. "To solitude."

She clinked her glass against his. "To being together."

"I meant solitude for us."

She sipped, then looked at him over the rim of her glass. "Did you?"

Sometimes he felt intimately connected with her, as though she was the only person in the world who truly understood him. Other times, like now…he had no idea what she was talking about.

He took a bracing sip of the drink, which, thanks to the premium clear tequila, was smooth and lime-infused. "You don't want Davis interrupting again, do you?" he asked.

"No. Are you sure he's not the reason you're here with me?"

"You've lost me."

"Am I some kind of prize in a competition between you and Davis?"

7

"OF COURSE NOT," Aidan said, looking annoyed.

Sloan narrowed her eyes. "I'm not interested in playing any macho crap games."

"Me, either. Though, as I recall, you were the one who wanted me to fight him for you last night."

"I didn't want you to fight. I wanted to know…well, I wanted to know if I mattered. If you…liked me."

His lips tipped upwards. "Why didn't you just pass me a note during study hall?" He grabbed her arm when she started to turn away. "You seem like a woman who knows when a guy is attracted to her."

"I am," she said firmly, meeting his gaze. "Usually, anyway. But you seem to be an exception. I can't figure out what you think."

He stepped close. His silver eyes darkened, smoky with unmistakable desire. "I think you're amazing. I think we have great chemistry. I know I like touching you. I like you touching me. Beyond that…" He shrugged.

Did they need anything beyond that? she wondered.

No.

She didn't want to get seriously involved, to have her heart and emotions tangled. Davis was a living—and now suddenly present—reminder of the pain she'd gone through when he left. She didn't want to give any man that kind of power over her again.

"That's enough." She smiled at him. "Now, let's get cooking. I'm starved." She turned toward the counter.

He grabbed her hips and pulled her back against him. "What kind of cooking—exactly?" he asked, low and sexy in her ear.

"The food kind." She glanced at him over her shoulder. "For now, anyway."

Thankfully, he decided to remove himself from temptation and install the lock while she worked on the tacos. A while later, despite the hunger they shared for each other and the tension-filled way things had ended between them the night before, the atmosphere during dinner was easy and comfortable.

They talked about their childhoods—his conservative, conventional one, her somewhat odd one. He'd walked to the neighborhood school; she'd ridden in a patrol car.

He'd raced his bike with his buddies; she'd shared her knowledge of investigative techniques, home safety and the dangers of firearms with her friends. He'd had babysitters when his parents went out to dinner; she'd been dropped off at the nunnery when her father had to attend an important meeting with the mayor or was sent out of town for a law-enforcement convention.

"I've definitely gotten the impression that you have the protector gene," Aidan said as he rinsed the dishes.

She'd cooked, so he'd insisted on cleaning up. Sister Mary Katherine would be impressed.

She came and stood next to him. "A protector gene?"

"Yeah. You make sure everybody feels welcome. You organize people, give them a purpose." He lifted his eyebrows. "You make sure everybody eats properly."

"It's called being nice."

"It's more than that. Why did you come back last night?"

"I wanted to be certain you were okay. A neighborly kind of thing," she added defensively. She'd just got through telling herself—and him—that she didn't need feelings getting in the way of their attraction.

"We're not neighbors."

"Then it was a fellow citizen thing." She scowled at him. "You didn't even invite me to lie down on your couch before you started psychoanalyzing me."

He dried his hands on a towel, then slid his arm around her waist. "Then let's do that." He led her to the den, where he flopped back onto the pillow-strewn couch.

Though he looked sexy as hell, with an inviting smile on his lips, his long, lean body all stretched out, she planted her hands on her hips. She wasn't that easy. "Why do I have the feeling getting me horizontal was your goal all along?"

He grabbed her hand and tumbled her on top of him. "Because it was."

Before she could say a word or get her breath back, his mouth was on hers. He slid his hand through her hair and cupped the back of her neck, angling her face as his tongue slid past her lips.

Pleasure sparked, then spread like a wildfire down her body. She sighed into him and spread her hands against his chest, feeling his heart hammer beneath her palms.

So she could be a little easy.

She wanted to melt into him, to absorb his energy and sensual nature, even his darkness and pain. She wanted this heat, the hunger and anticipation, to overwhelm her, draw her closer and make them one.

He moved his hand down her back, cupping her butt, pressing the length of their bodies tightly together. The fire in her veins spiked hotter, the flames flicking against her skin. She wanted him naked beneath her. Or over her.

She worked her hands beneath his T-shirt, and the feel of his bare, warm skin made her groan. He moved his hands between their bodies to cup her breasts.

And still the kiss went on.

She longed to say things, to tell him how much she wanted him, to tell him where to touch her—though he was doing pretty well without direction.

Lifting her mouth from his, she stared down at him—well, specifically his mouth. "Aidan, I…"

He made a visible effort to catch his breath. "Too much?"

It was the barriers between them bothering her. Emotions. Secrets. Clothes. And since only one of those was easy to deal with, she decided to go down the easy road.

For the moment, anyway.

"Not enough." Sitting up, straddling him, she grabbed the edge of her shirt and pulled it up and off. She helped him do the same with his.

They both unhooked her bra, then they fell back to the cushions, on their sides, belly-to-belly. Their hands were greedy with need and curiosity. His lips traced a path down the side of her neck as she clutched him, her breathing hitching as his mouth found her breast, his tongue brushing her nipple.

He thought she'd come here to comfort him, to protect him, and, on some level, maybe she had. But, really, she'd come for exactly this.

For desire to scream in her blood. For a man to remind her she wasn't just a librarian, or the sheriff's efficient and caretaking daughter or a woman who merely flirted instead of experiencing.

When he kissed his way down to her stomach, she shivered. She clenched her hands in his hair and arched closer. She craved his touch. Everywhere.

He unbuttoned her jeans, then shoved them down her hips. His finger slid past her belly button to the heat between her legs, gliding to her hot, wet center. She angled her hips upward, and his finger penetrated deeper, delving inside her, sending pulses of pleasure shooting everywhere.

Then his mouth was on hers, his tongue tangling with hers as her hips pumped against his hand. The pleasure spread, leaving her stomach trembling, her spine tingling.

With anxious hands, she unbuttoned his fly, then curled her hand around his erection. She slid her hand up and down him as he pushed his fingers inside her, mimicking the movements they both wanted in more intimacy.

"Damn," he breathed harshly in her ear. "Sloan, I…condoms."

Smiling, she glided her thumb across the top of his penis. "Where would we get them in Palmer's Island this time of night?"

He groaned. "I have no idea."

"We could go on like this."

His erection jerked in her hand as she moved down again. "Not for long."

She kissed the base of his throat, feeling his pulse pound, hard and strong, against her lips and felt giddy with expectation. "Who's the most efficient woman you know?"

"I— What? How should I—" He angled his head so that he could meet her gaze. "What're you up to?"

She flicked her tongue across his bottom lip. "How much do you want me?"

"I think you can feel how much." The tip of his finger

brushed her clitoris, and her whole body tightened with need. "How much do you want me?"

Gasping, she somehow managed to say, "Reach into my back pocket."

When he found the foil-wrapped packages, he dangled them above her before ripping one open with his teeth and tossing the rest aside. She helped him roll on the protection, then they both kicked off their jeans.

Naked, he moved between her legs, and she wrapped her thighs around his hips.

He brushed her hair off her face as he stared down at her. "It's not the most romantic setting."

She clenched her thighs.

"It should be…better."

Arching her back, she moved so that he slid deeper inside.

He closed his eyes and sank all the way.

She dug her fingers into his butt. "That's perfect."

Full penetration energized both of them. Their bodies had found what they liked, and they wanted more. Moving together, Sloan met his thrusts, feeling the power and need of them all the way down to her toes.

Still, her peak hovered just out of reach. She pressed her hips up, holding the position as Aidan moved against her, and those few, intimate strokes sent her over the edge.

She gasped and arched her neck, brushing her hands down his sweat-slicked stomach. His climax followed hers seconds later, and he clutched her against him, her breasts pressed against his bare skin, sending even greater tingles of pleasure skating down her spine.

He collapsed on top of her, and their hearts thumped in wild union for several minutes.

"You came here to seduce me," he said finally, his head pillowed against her breast.

"Pretty much." She stretched her arms over her head, then exhaled a long, satisfied sigh as she stroked her fingers down his back. "Thanks."

"My pleasure." He turned his head, kissing her shoulder. "And you proved my point."

"Did I?"

"The protection gene."

A woman who carried condoms in the back pocket of her jeans hardly had a platform for an argument. "Okay, fine, you win."

He lifted his head and kissed her softly on the lips. "I certainly did." Sliding off her, he propped himself on his elbow, his fingers gliding up and down her arm. "I have a bed, you know."

"You do? I never did get the upstairs tour."

"Fortunately, the tour guide is ready and available."

She felt at home and outside herself at the same time. Beyond his issues and her issues, and neither of them wanting to get involved, they were involved. At least she was. And even though she didn't want to look into his eyes and feel the fluttery craziness she did, the reaction was there anyway.

Plus, the alternative was loneliness and resentment. She'd had enough of that, and suspected he had, as well.

"You want to go up?" he asked when she remained silent.

She brushed her hand across his cheek. "I'd planned to seduce you slowly, with a dance and some soulful blues."

"You still can."

He reached across her and snagged his jeans off the floor. Scooting off the sofa, he stood and pulled on the pants, while she drifted into a lustful haze over his body. No man who spent ten to twelve hours behind a desk could look like that.

Had a few weeks of carpentry really honed him so amazingly?

After helping her stand, he tugged his T-shirt over her head. "Let me find my iPod."

As he walked away, she stuck her arms through the T-shirt's sleeves, and since it didn't quite cover her ass, she searched through her discarded clothes to find her panties, then put them on.

Glancing around the den, which she'd barely noticed until now, she flipped on a lamp and realized this room was an eclectic mix of old and new. The comfy sofa she and Aidan had put to such pleasurable and convenient use had modern lines and was covered in chocolate-colored fabric. A large mahogany cabinet in the corner was obviously an antique, but held a huge plasma-screen TV. There were antique end tables and modern lamps and a large wood-burning fireplace.

But there were no knickknacks or pictures. No hint of soul and spirit.

Would Aidan add pieces of himself? Would he hang around long enough to make this house a home? Or would his corporate-playboy side grow bored with sleepy Palmer's Island and want to move on after the renovations were completed?

He returned with his iPod and a small set of speakers, which he set on one of the end tables. He must have gone upstairs to get the system, since he wore a T-shirt, as well.

"Should I put on my jeans?" she asked, suddenly feeling naked.

"Hell, no." He flipped on the sound, and a bluesy guitar filled the room. He approached her, then pulled her into his arms and cupped her backside in his hands. "This is much better."

She wrapped her arms around his neck. "You put a shirt on."

His fingers skated across her lace-covered butt. "You put on panties." He lifted her shirt and peeked over her shoulder. "Let me see."

"You've seen pretty much everything."

"We stripped down too quickly." He held her at arm's length. "Come on."

Sloan had no idea why she was embarrassed. She bought lingerie to make her feel sexy and desirable. She lifted Aidan's T-shirt to her waist then turned around slowly, picturing her skimpy white lacy panties and the white satin bow that sat at the top of her butt. "Satisfied?"

He yanked her against his chest and they rocked along with the soulful music. "Not nearly, but the memory of that bow will keep me warm all through the harsh winter."

"We don't have harsh winters on Palmer's Island, and we won't even have our version of winter for nine months."

He grinned. "Then it'll keep me hot all summer."

"You think the renovations will be done by that time?"

"Maybe."

"What then?"

"By then something will have broken, so I'll have to start the process all over."

"So you're planning to stay here indefinitely?"

"I guess. I haven't thought much about the future." He stared over her shoulder, but she could sense he was looking into his thoughts, not at the room. "I need to see through this project."

"Why?" she asked, and his gaze jerked to hers. "I mean, I'm glad you're bringing Batherton back to life, but why is it so important?"

He said nothing for a long while. "After my parents died, I realized the necessity of preserving the past."

There was more. But she wasn't going to push. One, because he'd probably push back, and two, because his work on the house was obviously tied to his parents in an emotional way that he either didn't want to acknowledge, or wasn't ready to share.

She laid her head on his shoulder. "That's good."

Without conversation, they continued to sway against each other and to the music. Sloan felt as comfortable with Aidan as with anyone in a long, long time. With all her friends, work schedule and charity projects, she sometimes still felt alone. Even with Davis, with their history and being the only man besides her father she'd ever loved, she'd always harbored doubts. Had Davis sensed that resistance? Was that why he'd left?

She wasn't sure why, but she'd always wondered if someone would come along and break through completely. Was Aidan that man? Or was she simply dazzled by their attraction?

Then he threaded his fingers through her hair, and she forgot about anything but the way he made her feel. "Do you mind if we talk about Pete for a minute?" he asked, tipping her chin up to meet his gaze.

"Oh." She'd rather have him kiss her, but she wasn't planning on going anywhere that night, so she could be patient. "Sure. What's on your mind?"

"Now that you're staring at my lips, something entirely different."

She pressed her mouth lightly to his. "We've got all night. Tell me what you're thinking about Pete."

He kissed her again, then wrapped his arms tightly around her as they rocked back and forth to the low, mournful song that flowed from the speakers. Somehow, it seemed appropriate for the discussion. "I found some of his equipment this morning in the parlor."

"Is that so strange? He was keeping it here, wasn't he?"

"Sometimes. But he'd told me he liked to spend Saturday mornings in his woodworking shop, and his favorite saw is here. I can't help but wonder if he came back for it and someone followed him."

She frowned. "Someone who wanted him dead?"

"Or to have it out with him. If he was really dating all those women…"

"Maybe somebody got tired of sharing." Betsy had suggested the same thing earlier, and Sloan still found it far-fetched. "Is that your theory as a professional playboy?" she asked Aidan, her tone teasing.

"*Former* playboy."

"Uh-huh." She certainly didn't want to share him, but she couldn't imagine getting homicidal over him dating someone else.

Well, probably not.

Regardless, the evidence didn't seem to back up Aidan's suggestion. "Pete looked as if he was in good shape," she continued. "It doesn't seem likely a woman could stab him multiple times without him resisting."

"Maybe he did resist."

"But there was no other blood found at the scene. No drops trailing out the door. No bloody towels found in the trash. For an emotional killer she had to have kept a cool head to clean up after defending herself."

"It's possible the first blow did the job. The rest could have been fury."

Sloan pursed her lips. *That* made a great deal of sense. "We need the autopsy results."

"The sheriff will give them to you?"

"Sure." She narrowed her eyes. "And don't even think

about telling me how inappropriate it is for a librarian to—"
She broke off and stepped out of his arms. "Wait. What if one
of the women he's dating isn't exclusive, either? What if she
has a boyfriend? And he didn't like sharing?"

"Also a possibility. And you're certainly more experienced
at motives than I am." He reached out and snagged her hand,
pulling her close. "Together, you think we can solve it?"

With heat shimmering off him, she felt the air around
them shift. She laid her hand on his chest. "Find out who
killed Pete?"

"That." He slid his thumb across her lips and heat spread
outward through her veins. "And why we want each other so
much."

She angled her head so that their mouths were an inch
apart. She inhaled the masculine scent of him, felt the subtle
ripple of muscles beneath her palm. "I'm in if you are."

The kiss started gently, with slow, exploring strokes. His
mouth could go from a hard line to a dazzling smile in the space
of minutes, and yet every time his lips touched hers, desire
flared and the world fell away. His touch, his scent, his body
surrounded her as thoroughly as the music's seductive notes.

"Come upstairs with me?" he asked when they parted.

She doubted there were very few places she wouldn't go
with him. "Love to."

WHEN THEY REACHED his bedroom, Aidan gave only a passing
thought to the front door he'd locked on his way up.

Normal routine for him. Serious business for Palmer's Island.

Along with the hunger and wonder and anticipation of
being with Sloan, a glimmer of doubt poked at him, accusing
him of bringing violence to this trusting town. He hadn't, of
course, but throughout the process of dealing with his grief,

he'd come to acknowledge that many times forces moved in the world with a purpose.

Had his self-absorption really led to his parents' deaths?

Many times he thought that was true.

Then Sloan pulled her T-shirt—actually his T-shirt—over her head, dropping it on the floor, and he pushed anything but her from his mind.

The only illumination in the room came from the big arched window overlooking the backyard, through which the moonlight shone. She looked like an angel or a moon goddess, bare except for those enticing lace panties, her pale hair long and curving around her chest, nearly touching her nipples.

What had he done to receive this gift? And how could he hold on to it?

She approached him slowly, her lips curved in an inviting smile. She grasped the edge of his T-shirt, then worked it up his chest and over his head. Tracing one finger from the base of his throat to his waist, she asked, "Did you really get this body with carpentry?"

"Did I—what?"

"It's pretty amazing. I wonder if that was the reason Pete was so popular."

"Pete, huh?" He captured her finger. "You and he didn't…"

"You mean was I one of his harem?" She curled her arms around his neck and kissed his jaw. "No. I just figured you aren't in this good a shape because you sit behind a desk all day."

"You studied my body?"

"You stared at my ass."

"It's a really great ass."

She slid her hands down his back, gripping his backside briefly before she moved around to his stomach, where she started unbuttoning his jeans. "Same goes. You work out, I guess."

He nearly choked. "I, ah…run."

Her hand gripped the hard length of him as her tongue traced a line down the center of his chest. "Why are you so perfect?" she whispered.

I'm not was his automatic reaction. But with each touch, each word, she made him think he might get there.

She knelt in front of him, freeing his erection from his jeans and taking him into her mouth.

Though he wasn't running anywhere tonight. He tangled his hands in her hair and ground his teeth against exploding. He might not deserve the exquisite pleasure she offered, but he was taking it anyway. What kind of man that made him, he wasn't sure.

But he could only take so much.

He grabbed her arms and dragged her upward, covering her mouth with his and pouring all the heat and need bubbling inside him directly into her. Rubbing her bare chest against his, she cupped his face and moaned as he backed her to his bed.

The king-size replica antique four-poster, complete with gauzy white curtains dangling above the rails, had seemed like a caught-up-in-historical-accuracy moment when he'd bought it, but pressing Sloan into the mattress, watching her hair fan out and standing between her open thighs made him sure he'd done the right thing. For once since they'd met, he'd set the stage properly. A goddess belonged in a lord-of-the-manor bed.

Wildly grateful she'd grabbed several more condom packets before they'd come upstairs, he rolled on the protection, then stripped off her panties and entered her in one smooth stroke. She gasped and arched her back.

He wrapped her legs around his waist and slid his hands

up her stomach, her skin so soft and delicate. As he cupped her breasts, her nipples puckered, so he took one in his mouth, all the while moving in and out of her body, which gripped him like a silken fist.

Pleasure raced down his spine. The spicy, exotic island fruit scent she wore rose from her skin and wrapped itself around him, seducing him, urging him to drive them both to ecstasy.

Her fingers dug into his shoulders, and her breath was coming in short, almost desperate pants. His own climax was begging to explode. Still, he wanted more, he wanted to rock inside her endlessly, he wanted to feel her hunger for him, to know he made her feel amazing.

But when she moaned low in her throat, and her body clenched around his erection, his willpower was shattered. He pumped his hips and surged to the peak with her, finally crumpling into her when the powerful, blissful vibrations subsided.

Stroking her hair, he hoped his weight wasn't too much for her. He wasn't sure he could move.

And it was that moment when he realized he was standing on the floor and technically still had his jeans on.

He squeezed his eyes shut. He'd actually complimented himself on setting the stage right this time. *Good job, Kendrick.*

His only defense? When he touched her his mind turned into a tunnel, with her as the only light. His entire world was centered on her pleasure and his.

Could he tell her that without sounding cheesy?

"I'm sorry," he mumbled, lifting himself off her and shifting them both so that they were lying side-by-side on their backs.

"Sorry?" she asked, her breathing still labored.

"Earlier I'm fumbling like a teenager on the couch, and now I don't even bother to get undressed."

"I don't remember any fumbling." She stroked her hand down his side, then tugged on the belt loop of his jeans. "And you look really hot in those jeans."

Even when he was screwing up, she made him feel like a hero. How incredible was that?

"It's not very romantic," he said.

"It's *real*." She rolled to her side, propping herself on her elbow, laying her other hand on his chest. "When you touch me, I forget everything but you, the way you make me feel. I want you to get carried away, to need to be inside me so badly that you don't bother getting undressed. I certainly don't need a prelit stage and rehearsed lines."

Impressed by her—as always—he stroked her cheek. "You can definitely give an explanation without sounding cheesy."

"Sure I—" Confusion jumped into her eyes. "Huh?"

"I thought the same thing. I just wasn't sure how to explain the way I completely lose myself when I'm with you."

She smiled. "You do?"

He moved his hand to the back of her head, bringing her face close to his. "Oh, yeah."

Their lips met, and she expelled a satisfied sigh. The exploration was gentle, unhurried. Usually, after a date and sex, he was ready to be alone, to sleep or watch TV. But he didn't want Sloan more than an inch away. Even closer, if possible. Her scent, the way she moved, the way she kissed were all becoming familiar.

The connection he had with her was something he needed. He, the man who was trying so hard to be alone, not to rely on anyone, needed someone.

Sloan.

They parted, but he didn't let go. "Can you stay?"

Her face hovering over his, she met his gaze, her blue

eyes bright and focused. On him. "I can. The library's closed on Sunday."

"Do you make breakfast as well as you make tacos?"

"I'm legendary for my ham and cheese omelet."

Jealousy punched through him. "Legendary with whom?"

"The cops at the station house. I've been known to drop by on Saturday mornings."

"I have ham and cheese."

"So you do." She kissed him lightly and threaded her fingers through his hair. "You really want to find out what happened to Pete, don't you?"

Though the change in topic threw him for a moment, it somehow seemed right with her. And he wasn't sure how she knew, but was glad she did without him having to explain the emotions and instincts and details he wasn't ready to talk about. "Yeah, I do."

She curled his arm around her and tucked her back to his front. "Then we will."

8

AIDAN woke to pounding.

Pressing his face into his pillow, he fought to ignore the hammer echoing in his head. He'd only had one blessed drink last night.

"Are you gonna answer the door?" Sloan asked sleepily, tangling her legs with his.

He opened his eyes. "The door?"

"The one that somebody's pounding on." She tucked her head beneath his chin. "I think it's the front."

A warm, naked Sloan or some yahoo at the front door?

No contest there. Aidan slid his hand around her back, pulling her firmly against him, sucking in a breath when her bare breasts brushed his chest.

Pushing aside her tangled hair, he trailed his lips along her jaw. Now that he was awake, he couldn't think of any better way to spend a Sunday morning.

Ding-dong.

"You've got to be kidding," he murmured, lifting his head as his temper fired.

Sloan's fingers crawled up his chest. She kissed his chin. "They'll go away."

Moving his hand along her thigh, he hooked her leg over his hip. He could already feel the heat pumping off her skin.

He slid his hand down her body, finding her damp with need as his fingers delved between her legs.

Ding-dong.

True to his single-minded focus when he and Sloan were together, he blocked out the interruption. He drank in her sighs and concentrated on pleasuring her. His own body was throbbing, but he watched the flush of desire spread across her face as her eyes fluttered closed.

She clenched her hand around his arm when he found the button that would send her need soaring. But he intended to satisfy the ache that followed.

He flicked his finger against her. Light, teasing touches that brought a low moan from her throat. When he increased his pace, her breath hitched, and he pushed his fingers inside her to feel the rhythmic pulsing of her climax.

Before she could fully come back to herself, he moved between her legs and slid inside.

Her eyes flew open; she braced her hands at his waist.

And held on.

Gritting his teeth against the overwhelming need to explode, he drove her back up, hanging on the edge himself. Their passion rose quickly together, and he knew, with the scent and feel and visual of her surrendering to him all merging together, he couldn't last long.

So the minute she gasped and clenched her hips around him, he climaxed, and he clutched her against his sweat-slicked chest, absorbing the echoes of pleasure that rippled out like waves on the water.

Exhausted and exhilarated at the same time, he dragged his mouth down her throat, feeling her pulse race beneath his lips. "With a little more practice, we might get good at that."

"Yeah." She drew a deep breath, then exhaled. "Absolutely. Let's practice as much as—"

Ding-dong, ding-dong.

Aidan groaned. "Oh, come *on.*"

"Apparently they're not going away." Her hand suddenly tightened at his waist. "What if it's my dad?"

He flopped on his back. "Then you should answer it."

She fluffed her pillow. "It's *your* house."

"It's probably *your* casserole-toting friends."

She skimmed her fingers—slowly—across his stomach. "Are we having our first fight already?"

Even though the tone of her voice was put-upon seduction, and probably stemmed from sheer laziness and the lack of sleep they both suffered from, he responded. The sooner he got rid of the intruder, the sooner he could get back in bed with sexy Sloan.

"We're not fighting." With a resigned sigh, he tossed back the covers and wondered where the hell he'd left his jeans last night. Finding them in a heap on the floor, he jerked his body into them. If anybody but that nun—or the cute computer geek with the glasses—was on his doorstep, the sheriff was going to be investigating a new murder.

"Aidan?" when he glanced back, Sloan was sitting up in bed, the sheet tucked beneath her arms, her breasts peeking over the top. "I'll be waiting right here."

Aroused *and* annoyed, Aidan stalked into the hall.

Nuns, vulnerable teenagers, fathers or kindly neighbors—it didn't matter. Whoever had caused this interruption was getting booted.

At least Sloan had had the sense to bring a lock, and he'd had the urge to install it. Otherwise, they'd probably have half the town storming into the bedroom.

Aidan flung open the door and found Davis on the other side.

He closed his eyes and willed the other man away, but when he opened them, Davis was still standing there, looking pale and worried. "You've got to be kidding."

"I wanted to apologize."

"Apology accepted." Aidan started to close the door.

Davis grabbed the edge. "Can I come in?" He raised his hand to his head. "Pete's dead. What the hell happened the other night?"

Aidan crossed his arms over his chest and made an effort to look stern. "Have you come to confess to murder?"

"No." Davis shook his head violently. "No, of course not. But the last thing I remember before you shoving me awake yesterday was whiskey at Velma's. I have no idea what happened in between."

After the "he has conquests" accusation by Davis on Friday night, Aidan had a brief urge to tell the other man that in a drunken stupor he'd hired four strippers who'd tried to seduce him, but found their client lacking in motivation and equipment, so they'd decided to move on to a more interesting guy.

"You slept," Aidan said finally. "We came back here, where we found Sloan, who'd found Pete's body. The sheriff came. The coroner came. They left. I pulled you inside. End of story."

"And Pete?"

"Somebody stabbed him." Aidan had no intention of going into the details with Davis. Let him read about the crime in the biweekly paper. "Look, I've got somebody upstairs. We can talk later in the week."

Davis's head jerked up. "You move fast."

"When I can."

A look of triumph flashed across Davis's face. "I told Sloan you did. She's no match for a guy like you."

Okay, that's just irritating.

Aware of his rumpled, bare-chested appearance, Aidan leaned against the doorframe. "She matches me just fine."

Davis's smile faded. "The somebody upstairs is Sloan."

Aidan simply nodded.

Pain flashed across Davis's face. "She won't even return my phone calls."

Aidan wasn't sure what to say to that. He wasn't trying to throw his relationship with Sloan in the guy's face.

Well, not too much.

"You guys have history," he said finally. "And not an entirely smooth one."

"Yeah." Davis tunneled his hand through his hair. "My fault. But you'd think she'd at least listen to my apology. She won't even think about giving me a second chance. She's so caught up in—" He stopped and stared at Aidan. "She's so caught up in you."

"Look, I—"

"Aidan?"

Aidan turned to see Sloan, wearing his robe, and walking down the steps. Could this whole deal get more awkward? Of course, if Davis would stop dropping by uninvited and unannounced...

"Who's at the door? What's taking so—" She stopped, obviously catching sight of Davis. "What are you doing here?" she asked, stomping down the last few steps. She crossed her arms over her chest as she faced her ex.

"I came to talk to Aidan," he explained, his gaze darting from Aidan to Sloan and back again. Shock and embarrassment were evident in his eyes. "Obviously, I came at a bad time. I'll go."

Sloan grabbed his arm. "I didn't mean to—"

"It's not your fault," Davis said, sliding his thumb across her cheek. "I'm the jerk, right?"

"No—well, sometimes." She stepped back, out of his reach.

Which was a good thing, because Aidan was tempted to break his hand.

"Let's have lunch tomorrow, okay?" she continued to Davis.

"Okay."

"Mabel's at twelve-thirty?"

"Sounds good." Davis's gaze moved to Aidan. "Sorry to interrupt." He waved, then moved down the sidewalk toward his car.

Sloan's words about Davis from a few days ago came back to Aidan at that moment. *Why that man, of all the others, could always hit me right here...*

If Davis really crawled, if he gave the sales pitch Aidan knew he was capable of, would she take him back?

Their relationship had obviously been a turning point in her life. How exactly did she feel about Davis now? Could one night with Aidan really overshadow all that she and her ex had shared in the past?

Making an effort to put his worries aside, he stroked her back. "Are you okay?"

"Sure."

"You're having lunch."

She turned, meeting his gaze. "Sorry. I guess that was a little weird. It's not a date. I just need to talk things out with him."

He wanted to tell her she could date Davis if she wanted, that they hadn't made any promises, but he couldn't force the words out. "It's fine. I guess you didn't expect him to be so..."

"Upset." She sighed. "No, I didn't. Mostly, I thought this was a pissing contest with you." She held up her hand to stop his protest. "On his part, not yours. And I really wish I was glad to hurt him. He certainly hurt me."

"But you're not."

She shook her head. "I don't know what I am. Except hungry." She linked hands with him. "How about that omelet?"

Aidan wanted to know more about the relationship between her and Davis, but he could hardly ask probing questions when his own past was a subject he didn't want anything to do with.

WEARING a bright yellow sundress, white cropped jacket and white patent leather sandals, Sloan walked into Mabel's at precisely twelve-thirty the next day.

When a woman was meeting her ex, who'd unceremoniously dumped her, and who now clearly wanted her back while she was having a hot and heavy affair with his former boss, she could be as bold and confident as she liked.

"You're dressed up," Courtney said, bumping shoulders with her as she headed toward the door with a large bag, probably lunch for her stylists.

Sloan flipped her hair over her shoulder. "It's a lovely spring day."

"And Davis Curnan is sitting in the far corner booth."

"Is he?"

She grinned. "So you've already introduced yourself to the infamous rich guy in town, plus you're juggling your ex *and* solving the Crime of the Decade?"

"Of course." Turning serious, she laid her hand on Courtney's arm and lowered her voice. "Have you heard anything about Pete's personal life?"

"He got around, that's for sure. Last year, there was even a pushing match between Pete and Marla Henson's husband."

"I don't know them."

"The official story was that John Henson didn't like the deck Pete built behind their house." Courtney shook her head. "But one of my stylists does Marla's hair, and she swears Marla was bragging about much more than Pete's carpentry skills."

Sloan suppressed a groan. The more questions she asked, the more suspects she got.

"Any luck with Aidan Kendrick and the historical committee brochure?" Courtney asked.

Sloan coughed. In the light of Pete's murder and her own carnal adventures, she'd forgotten all about the brochure. "Ah, no. Finding Pete pretty much shifted our committee goals to the backseat."

"Naturally." Courtney glanced around to be sure they weren't being overheard. "Was it really gruesome?"

Sloan didn't want to remember the vibrant, charming carpenter the way she'd found him. Yet, if it wasn't for the distraction of Aidan and the pleasure he offered, she was sure she'd never be able to close her eyes without reliving the moment of discovering Pete's blood-soaked body.

"It was bad," she said finally.

Courtney squeezed her hand. "Call me if you need anything. I know it's going to be hard on you and the sheriff."

Sloan worked up a smile. "We'll manage."

They said their good-byes, and Sloan headed across the restaurant. As she approached Davis's table, he rose, then brushed his lips across her cheek.

"You look lovely," he said.

"Thanks."

As she scooted past him into the booth, he commented, "It looks like we're the featured attraction."

Sloan didn't need to look around the busy restaurant to know she and Davis were being watched by most of the diners.

"I'd forgotten about the lack of privacy in a small town," Davis continued.

Sloan hadn't. Maybe she shouldn't let her pride rule her decisions, but she wanted anybody nosy enough to see her with Davis. To see she wasn't still mooning over him. She'd moved on and gotten over—

She stopped, realizing suddenly it was true. She was over Davis.

And while some of her confidence stemmed from her relationship with Aidan, the rest was simply inside her.

She'd been hurt, badly, but she'd pulled herself together, left the past behind and gotten on with her life. Davis's appearance in town didn't change that.

"I got you some tea," Davis said, sliding one of Mabel's signature blue plastic glasses in front of her and drawing her out of her thoughts.

"Thanks." She took a sip, then met Davis's gaze. "I'm sorry everything was so awkward for you yesterday."

"Yeah, me, too. I was surprised, I guess. I mean, I knew Kendrick moved fast, but not that fast."

She narrowed her eyes. "This lunch is going to be over in a big hurry if you plan to spend it warning me away from Aidan."

"You won't respect my opinion, even though I've known him longer and know him better than you do?"

"You don't—"

"Hey," the waitress, Daphne, said, appearing by the table, "I haven't seen you two together in here in a long time."

"Davis moved to Atlanta, remember?" Sloan said.

"Oh, that's right," she said, then sighed. "Such a shame about you two. Everybody figured y'all would be married with a couple of kids by now."

"Did they?" Sloan glanced down at her menu, then back at Daphne. "I'll have the flounder, collard greens and macaroni and cheese."

"Does this mean you're movin' back, Davis?" Daphne asked slyly as she tucked Sloan's menu beneath her arm.

"I'm just visiting. For now."

He gave Daphne his order, and though she tried to probe further about what he was doing in town and how long he was staying, his vague answers obviously frustrated her enough that she gave up.

"I'm beginning to appreciate the anonymity of Atlanta more and more," Davis said as Daphne walked away.

"In light of Pete's death, I don't think we'll be the big story for long." She sipped her tea. "And I thought you liked being popular."

"Our relationship isn't anyone's business but ours."

"I agree. Yet you think mine and Aidan's is."

He looked annoyed—no doubt from being caught by his own words. "I'm concerned about you."

"As a friend, or as my ex?"

"Both."

"You don't know Aidan at all."

"I know he's hard. And ruthless."

She was well aware of that. But there was also a softness and vulnerability in him that spoke directly to her. Maybe she was, in fact, the only one who saw it.

"I don't want to see you get involved with somebody like him," Davis continued.

Sloan angled her head. "It's too late for that, don't you think?"

"You didn't sleep with me for two months after we started dating."

She leaned back in the booth, eyeing him closely, feeling her temper start to simmer. "So he got me in bed sooner, and your ego is bruised?"

"I guess it is."

Their plates arrived, so they ate in silence for a few minutes. Thinking rationally, Sloan could sympathize with Davis's feelings. She sure hadn't felt all hot and sexy when he'd told her he was attracted to a woman from his office and wanted to break up. And, unlike him, she hadn't shown up on his doorstep and found him rumpled from an obviously carnal night and wearing the other woman's bathrobe on a Sunday morning.

"It's not like you—to trust someone you barely know," Davis said, adding salt to his mashed potatoes. "Especially after Pete's been murdered."

"What does Aidan have to do with Pete's death?"

Davis's gaze held hers. "You tell me."

Sloan was tempted to toss aside her napkin and leave. "Surely you're not accusing him of stabbing Pete to death? *You're* his alibi."

"I don't really remember a lot," he said, then waved his hand when she glared at him. "I'm not accusing him of anything. But it did happen in his house, while Pete was working for him. He's intimately involved in the case."

"So am I."

Davis scoffed. "You're not going to go all teen sleuth on us, are you?"

"You never did appreciate my detective abilities."

"I can't imagine why," he said sarcastically. "Since they generally had you reading autopsy reports during our dinner dates."

"It was one autopsy report, and I can't help it if you have a weak stomach."

"At least you nursed me back to health." He smiled. "Sloan's special brand of TLC."

Which, she seemed to recall, involved her and some rather risqué lingerie.

And still, nothing she'd shared with him in the nearly two years they'd dated had ever matched her single night with Aidan. *Scary.* Scary and exciting at the same time.

He laid his hand over hers, threading their fingers and bringing her attention back to him. "It's over between us, isn't it?"

She squeezed his hand. "Yes." There were very few times in his life that Davis hadn't gotten exactly what he wanted, and whether he really wanted her back, or his life was simply going through a transition, she knew he would be hurt by her rejection. "I'm not angry at you anymore, Davis. I've just moved on. Truthfully, even when we were together, I had my doubts. Maybe you sensed those, maybe that's what drove you away."

"There were times I wasn't sure you were all the way with me, but I had my own issues. I felt like I was suffocating here." He glanced around the familiar and, to her, beloved restaurant. "I wanted new challenges. I wanted to see if I could be a success in the big city."

"And you are."

"Was. Kendrick selling his company was a pretty big setback."

"It was hard for him, too, but he has his reasons."

"Yeah? What are they?"

She shook her head. "Personal." She wasn't even sure

herself, though she was beginning to get a glimmer. "Just as you needed to get out of here, he needed to get out of Atlanta."

"He won't stay here, Sloan. And you won't ever leave."

She shrugged. She certainly wouldn't ever leave her hometown, and Aidan might get bored after a while. Maybe the heat between them would burn out quickly. Maybe this whole thing would blow up in their faces.

She just didn't give a damn.

"What if he breaks your heart?" Davis asked, his voice full of true concern.

"I'll get over it." She patted his hand. "I got over you, didn't I?"

AIDAN HAMMERED.

And he didn't watch the clock. At least not the antique grandfather clock. That's what wristwatches were for.

Eventually, he knew he'd have to replace Pete, but since that decision seemed incredibly morbid, and for now he had enough work he could do alone, he was getting it done.

The baseboard trim in the dining room had already been stained, so he'd spent the morning nailing it in place. He'd found a dining-room table through an antique dealer in Georgia, and he planned to ask Sloan for recommendations for a local teenager or handyman who could drive over to Savannah and get it.

Sloan.

She'd left Sunday afternoon—reluctantly, he liked to think—and he hadn't seen or talked to her since. But that didn't mean he hadn't thought about her.

Nearly every minute.

He glanced at his watch. Twelve forty-five.

She was with Davis now. What was he telling her? What was she saying to him? Was she touching him? Even the thought of her skin in contact with Davis's hands made his blood boil.

And you, Aidan Kendrick, are officially pathetic.

He set aside his hammer and released a long breath. They'd made no commitment to each other besides finding Pete's killer, but he couldn't rid himself of the idea that she belonged to him. Davis had had his chance, and—fool that he was— had blown it.

Aidan forced himself to go back to work. After another couple of hours, he glanced at his cell phone, lying nearby on a sawhorse.

He had been wondering some things about Pete that morning. Namely, about his business practices. For all his easygoing attitude, he had to have some business savvy. He had suppliers and clients.

Did he pay his bills regularly? Were any of his clients angry or dissatisfied?

Sloan would know. Or could find out.

He wanted to convince himself that his need to talk to her was all about Pete's death and the investigation they'd agreed to collaborate on. But while that was a big part of his thoughts, he simply wanted to see her. Touch her.

Giving in to temptation, he scooped up his phone and, mindful of the silence required in the library, sent her a text message. *Can you come by later?*

He stuck his cell phone in his jeans pocket, then walked into the kitchen for a bottle of water. He'd barely swallowed two sips before his phone beeped with an incoming message.

Sure. Is something wrong?

No. Just want to talk about Pete. He also wanted to know what had happened at lunch, plus he just plain missed her.

Okay. Should I bring dinner?

He grinned. The woman was determined to make sure he was well fed. His mother used to do the same thing. *I'll take care of it,* he sent back.

Be there at six.

His fingers hesitated over the minikeyboard, but in the end he resisted adding something mushy and laid the phone on the counter. He didn't really do mushy. He was supposed to be Lonely Guy Hiding in the Dark, after all.

The fact that he was tempted to be mushy, though, was telling.

Drinking water, he wandered out of the kitchen, then through the first-floor rooms. There were new light fixtures, sanded and stained floors, bathrooms with new tile. He'd bought dozens of antique accessories and pieces of furniture.

History was coming back to life. Maybe he was, as well.

People in Palmer's Island who appeared on his doorstep unannounced still made him leery. Even more disturbing was their obvious lack of worry about his lack of welcome. It was as if they knew he'd accept them eventually, provided they kept showing up with food.

And while that technique had worked for Sloan, she was a unique, hot and sexy case. Everybody else needed to keep their distance.

Not that they were doing so.

He'd already gotten two calls that day from Penelope—who apparently ruled the library at her school and was allowed to use the phone whenever she liked. He'd answered her questions about his new laptop. She checked with him about speed, screen size, memory and prices, then she'd called back twenty minutes later with delivery information and the appointment with the computer technician—her—who'd set up everything, including the super-fast T1 connection for the Internet.

After one meeting and two phone calls, Aidan was convinced Penelope would rule the world someday.

The rest of the afternoon, he nailed baseboards, sanded the columns in the library, made a run to the grocery store for steaks and the home improvement store for a grill and even swept the parlor. He glanced at Pete's equipment several times and wondered what he should do with it. He doubted his family wanted it shipped back to California and decided to offer to buy it. With all the work yet to be done, he'd need it, and something positive needed to come from the tragedy.

Why hadn't he considered that when his parents died?

He'd hounded the police, shunned the media, blamed all the wrong people, hoarded his anger and eventually shut himself away from everybody who wanted to help him.

Why hadn't he sponsored a neighborhood watch, or sunk some of the money he was so busy making into passing out flyers on the streets? Or called a press conference and offered a reward for information on the case? Or *helped* the police, instead of complaining to them?

His parents were intrinsic to his life; he'd barely known Pete.

But he was thinking clearly now, and it was inexcusable that he hadn't used the curiosity and publicity to help, rather than shut himself away from them.

Was Pete's death his do-over?

The doorbell rang, and he shoved aside his self-evaluation. The prospect of seeing Sloan was much more important.

His heart was pounding against his ribs as he crossed the hallway. He didn't want to be so transparently needy. But somehow between the first time she'd knocked on his door and now, he'd lost his scowls and barely-contained fury.

He was losing his defenses. And why didn't that bother him?

The moment he opened the door, he scented her, a mix of pineapples, sunshine and coconuts. He yanked her into his arms and covered her mouth with his.

9

PLASTERED AGAINST Aidan's chest, her head still spinning from the powerful kiss, Sloan tried to catch her breath. "That was some greeting."

Staring at her, he smoothed her hair off her face. "I mi—" He stopped and looked away.

"Missed me? Come on, you can admit it." She dropped her purse on the floor and curled her arms around his neck. "I missed you."

"I'm glad you're here."

She grinned. "Obviously."

He kissed her again, briefly, then linked their hands. "Come see what I bought today."

He led her down the hall, through the kitchen and out the back door. There, on the cracked concrete patio was a stainless-steel gas grill roughly the size of a 747. "Wow."

"As long as I was going to buy one, I figured I might as well buy the best."

"And the biggest."

"Naturally." He ran his hand across the shiny surface. "We'll break it in tonight. I bought steaks."

"Sounds good." In more ways than one. Didn't investing in a grill of that size signal he planned to cook out here for many years to come? Maybe he would be more amenable to helping out the historical society. Had they established enough trust between them? Or was she crazy to rock the boat on the balance and bond they'd managed to achieve?

Leading her back into the kitchen, he snagged a bottle of wine and a corkscrew off the counter. "I also have candles and a tablecloth." He nodded toward the table.

She glanced over to see that a white cloth covered it and cream-colored tapers in silver holders sat in the center. "You don't have to—"

"Yes, I do. It's important to me."

She was flattered, but she didn't want him to go too heavy into the romantic setting just yet. They still had the investigation to consider. And the people who'd be helping.

"Are you hungry? Should I start the grill?" he asked, opening the wine.

"Not quite yet. Some people may drop by."

"What people?"

He should know by now that everything was a community project, but she said, "Friends, other people who are concerned about Pete's death. It's still a small, discreet, very unofficial task force at this point."

Eyebrows raised, he handed her a glass of merlot. "Task force, huh? Do I want to know how that happened? I thought this was something you and I were going to discreetly investigate. I didn't get enough wine for everybody."

"I doubt they'll stay long, and it happened because it's hard to do anything discreetly in Palmer's Island. Plus, when our first murder in five years has happened, and I'm suddenly asking questions about the life and loves of the victim…"

"People put questions and Nancy Drew together, and come up with you."

She sipped her wine, but looked at him over the rim of the

glass. He wasn't smiling, but he wasn't scowling, either. The best she could probably hope for. "Exactly."

"Any particular reason they're coming here?"

"We had to have a headquarters somewhere."

Now, he scowled. "Headquarters?"

She patted his arm. "Gathering place. Drop-off point. It's not a big deal."

"I guess it's a good thing I ordered a dining-room table today."

"It couldn't hurt."

"By the way, do you know anybody I can hire to drive over to Savannah to pick it up?"

He took that awfully well. She was extremely nervous that this investigation was going to bring back memories of his parents' deaths. While she felt compelled to help, she didn't want that haunted look back in Aidan's eyes. Losing his parents had put it there, of course. Somehow—and she intended to find out how—he blamed himself for their deaths.

Penance. That's what he'd said he'd come to Palmer's Island for.

"I've got a truck they can use," Aidan continued, jerking her attention back to the present topic. "I just need somebody trustworthy to drive it."

"Oh, sure. I'll call Gus."

"Isn't he the guy who came over with the coroner the other night? The one who took away Pete's body?"

"That's him. He delivers furniture for the local stores by day."

"This is a very strange town."

"You'll get used to it."

Would he? No matter how dedicated Aidan was to the house, she had a hard time picturing him living in town way into the future. Davis was right about one thing—Aidan wouldn't stay.

He was a driven, ambitious man. He'd eventually need new challenges.

But then she and Aidan hadn't made any promises or commitments. That was the way they both wanted things. She'd only dealt with her issues over Davis that afternoon. She didn't need to get involved in a serious relationship.

"I guess I should have checked with you before offering your house," she said.

"I expect you didn't because you figured I'd refuse."

"The thought did cross my mind."

"I doubt anybody says no to you."

"Oh, they say it. They just don't mean it."

He lifted his hands. "The more the merrier."

"You don't mean that."

"No, I don't. But I'd rather them interrupt our date in the beginning, rather than the middle or end."

"Here, here." She clinked her glass against his. "At least we don't have to worry about Davis being the intruder."

His gaze locked with hers. "We don't?"

"No. We settled things between us. I told him I didn't want him coming over here, and I didn't want to hear anymore criticism of you and our relationship."

"So you're not going back to him?"

"No." She angled her head, trying to see if this news made him happy or if he didn't seem to care. "Did you think I was?"

"Davis can be pretty persuasive."

"But you're glad I'm not going to be seeing him?"

"Yes," he said—reluctantly it seemed to her. "I know it's none of my business, and normally I'm not a possessive man." His gaze searched hers. "You seem to be different."

She swallowed. "You, too."

"I'm not sure what it means, if anything." He cupped her jaw with his hand. "But I'm glad you're here."

She set her wineglass on the counter, then wrapped her arms around his waist. "And you missed me today. You *pined* for me all morning."

"How much will my next comment about that relate to my chances for getting you naked later?"

"There's a definite correlation," she said, teasing.

"Then not only did I miss you and pine for you, I wrote a poem to express my loneliness and despair. It's called 'An Ode to Hot Legs.' Wanna hear it?"

"I think I'll wait for *The Poetry Home Journal* to print it, so I can be surprised."

He sighed. "Okay, but you're really missing out."

It was hard to believe that barely a week ago there was truly an air of loneliness and despair about him, and tonight he was basically making fun of himself. As it had the moment he'd first smiled, her stomach fluttered in both pleasure and panic. If the man started being charming and *happy,* she was in serious doubt she could remain blasé about this relationship.

The doorbell rang, breaking into their teasing moment, but for once neither of them were upset by the interruption.

"You get the door," Aidan said. "I'll hide the wine."

Laughing, Sloan strode out. The visitors turned out to be Courtney and Helen.

"Autopsy report," Helen said, holding up a brown envelope. "Straight from the sheriff's office."

"Betsy and Patsy couldn't make it," Courtney said as they walked inside. "They're baking cookies for the middle-school playground-equipment fund-raiser."

"And Sister Mary Katherine didn't think it was appropriate to bring Penelope to this particular discussion." Helen sighed and laid her purse on the foyer table. "Thank goodness it's cool in here. I swear it went up to ninety today."

Courtney's gaze darted around the entry area. "Oh, my. Everything looks amazing." Her face flushed with excitement, she rushed toward the dining room and flipped on the light. "The chandelier, the detail on the woodwork…they're beautiful."

Helen ran her hand over the staircase banister, winding in a twist of iron and wood to the second floor. "He's really going to do the old place justice."

"I brought my camera." Courtney pulled it from her purse and waved it around. "We really need to document all this for the brochure and Web site."

"I'm not so sure—" Sloan began as Courtney snapped pictures. "What Web site?"

"The one Penelope is establishing," Helen said. "The way to keep history alive is to invest in the future. Or so she says."

Sloan hadn't cleared pictures, a Web site or a brochure with Aidan. Was the ad campaign spinning out of control before it had even begun?

She intended to promote the house to keep the historical society in the black. She intended to find Pete's killer to protect her town. And she suddenly wasn't sure if all that could happen at the same time.

"We should jump on the brochure," Courtney said. "Wouldn't it be nice to have them printed and distributed at the visitor's center in Charleston in time for the summer season? It's a shame, since the oyster roast is next weekend, we'll never have time to capitalize on that event."

"Don't mention the brochure." Sloan paused. "Or the Web site."

"You haven't talked to him about it yet?" Helen asked.

"I've barely known the man a week," Sloan said. "How

about we let him unpack his suitcases before we burden him with being responsible for saving the town's historical legacy?"

"I suppose that's true," Courtney replied.

Helen planted her hands on her hips. "You're the one who brought a camera."

"I'm going to take pictures *surreptitiously,*" Courtney said, her tone defensive. "So we'll be prepared when the time comes."

"Ladies," Sloan said, laying an arm around each of their shoulders. "Let's focus on Pete for now, okay?"

"You're right, of course," Courtney said, sliding her camera back in her purse. "I suppose it is a bit morbid to consider using a house where a murder has occurred as part of a publicity campaign."

Helen pursed her lips. "Morbid? Maybe so. Good publicity? Definitely."

"But Mr. Kendrick is okay with us having the meeting here?" Courtney asked. "You said he's really protective of his privacy."

Mr. Kendrick. A whole lot had happened since the last committee meeting at the library. It was going to be obvious to the other ladies that she and Aidan were more than new homeownder and historical-inspection designate. But she didn't want that to overshadow the work they needed to do.

"He's fine," Sloan said vaguely.

"The report says Pete was found at the base of the stairs." Helen, always quick to get to the point, walked in that direction. "Where, exactly?"

"Let me introduce you to our newest resident, then we'll get to the specifics. And we'll give you a full tour of the house."

They headed toward the hallway, only to be met by Aidan before they reached it. His gaze connected with Sloan's. "I was beginning to wonder if you'd gotten lost."

"We're here now," Sloan said, then performed the introductions. There was no doubt that Helen and Courtney were dazzled by Aidan—what woman wouldn't be, after all?

Leanly muscled in worn jeans and a fitted navy T-shirt, he looked sexy and dangerously casual. Her first instincts about him—as a wolf who could pounce suddenly—hadn't changed, even with all the intimate moments they'd shared.

Maybe because of them.

"Can I get you ladies something to drink?" Aidan asked when they reached the kitchen.

"Diet soda, if you have it," Courtney said, her face flushing as he pulled out a chair for her at the table. "Water if you don't."

"How about some wine?" asked Helen, who'd pulled out her own chair.

"No soda, but I have water and wine." He headed toward the fridge.

Sloan noticed Aidan didn't so much as blink at Helen's order, which only confirmed that he was a smooth operator when he wanted to be. Yet it never occurred to her that anything between them was fake or forced. As Davis had said, she didn't trust easily—at least not with really personal issues.

You seem to be different. Aidan's words were true in so many ways. They were both fiercely independent people who found themselves reliant on and wary of the other.

Helen nudged her arm. "Hot looks from the hot Mr. Kendrick?"

"Candles and a white tablecloth?" Courtney grinned knowingly. "Obviously, you're not just here to inspect the crown molding."

"It's complicated," was all Sloan could think to tell them.

Aidan brought back the drinks, and they gathered around

the table. A librarian, a real-estate agent, a hair stylist, a former communications mogul and two cookie-making experts in absentia were going to solve the island's Crime of the Decade. It might have been laughable if Sloan hadn't believed with all her heart that they would succeed.

An unconventional group, but a determined one. Though certainly assisted by the sheriff and his staff.

"So, let's get down to business," she said, pulling the autopsy reports from the envelope Helen had brought.

Helen had made several copies, so they all read silently for a few minutes. Sloan frowned over the coroner's conclusions, which were backed up by the state investigation unit. "A six-inch blade seems to be the murder weapon." Her gaze flicked toward Aidan. "That's more in line with a mugging. A street crime for whatever cash or valuables someone is carrying."

"Or a Boy Scout," Helen said.

Courtney's mouth formed an O. "That's not at all funny."

"I didn't mean it to be." Helen leaned forward. "How many Scout leaders do we have in town? How many skeletons are in their closets?"

"That is completely inappropriate," Courtney accused Helen.

"What does Scouting have to do with Pete?" Aidan asked reasonably.

Sloan was grateful for his insight. Courtney tended to get quickly offended by Helen's cynical—though brutally honest—assessment of every situation. "Plenty of people besides homicidal Scout leaders carry pocket knives," Sloan said. "Six inches isn't a samurai sword, it's a way to cut string or open boxes. Plenty of construction people, dock workers and salespeople at the hardware store carry knives. My dad keeps one in his glove box."

"Mine, too," Courtney said.

"Did Pete?" Helen asked, her gaze going to Aidan.

"I never saw one," he said. "When deliveries came to the house, I always grabbed scissors from the kitchen to cut open box strings or packages."

"John Henson is a Scout leader," Helen said abruptly.

Obviously, Courtney had told Helen about the incident between Pete and Marla Henson's husband from several months ago. Since Aidan was confused, Sloan explained about Marla's suspected affair with Pete, and the shoving-match confrontation between her husband and the carpenter.

Aidan rose and pulled a bottle of water from the fridge. "So, either Marla, the slutty housewife, or her husband, the Scout leader—or both—stalked Pete to my house and killed him?"

As ludicrous as the scenario seemed, nothing made sense. Maybe the answer lay in the obscure. Sloan didn't know the Hensons, so she had nothing personal to base her opinion on.

The evidence did tell them something important, though.

"The first blow did the job," she said quietly, feeling her stomach turn at the idea of the vibrant and talented Pete's life being snuffed out in that instant. "A woman could have done it. If she surprised him, and had any decent strength…"

She trailed off, and the group fell into silence once again. The importance of what they were discussing, regardless of the gossip generated in town, mattered to all of them for varying reasons, but simply by being present tonight they were bonded into being part of the solution

"If a woman *was* responsible," Courtney began, "it could have been any of the women Pete was involved with. Marla Henson wasn't exactly in an exclusive club."

Helen rose. "Let's get a look at the scene. Act out the possibilities."

"Act out?" Sloan said, glancing up at her friend.

"Sure." Helen grabbed one of the candles off the table. "This will be our weapon. We'll run through the scenarios and suppositions and try to match them with the evidence."

Courtney bit her lip, then rose to her feet. "It's not a bad idea."

Sloan, as usual, was worried about Aidan. There was no way this wasn't bringing back memories of his parents. "I don't know."

With a resigned sigh, Aidan stood. "Why do I have the feeling I'm playing Pete?"

Quietly, they gathered in the foyer.

Sloan showed them the spot where she'd discovered Pete's body. Aidan pointed out the proximity of his carpentry equipment in the parlor.

Courtney held up her hand. "So you think he came back here to get his tools? But what if he and Marla—or whoever— had come back here with the intention of romance rather than work? What if the location of his body and the tools doesn't matter at all?"

"She has a point," Helen said, her gaze sweeping the base of the stairs. "Maybe they were on their way upstairs when something happened. An intruder? Or a fight?"

Aidan shook his head. "Pete wouldn't have arranged a liaison with somebody here. He had no idea I'd be gone. I was nearly always here. Certainly at night." His gaze moved to Sloan. "That night was unusual."

"In what way?" Courtney asked. "Why did you leave?"

Sloan shook her head.

"If we're going to help, we need to know what happened that night," Courtney said, picking up on the idea that it was personal between Sloan and Aidan. "This isn't gossip. It's about Pete."

To Sloan's surprise, Aidan nodded. "Sloan and I were here having dinner." He paused. "Then Davis Curnan showed up."

Helen's eyes lit briefly before she doused the excitement. She cleared her throat. "I bet he wasn't happy."

"No." Aidan took a seat on the stairs. "Sloan left. Davis and I went to Velma's."

"But *you* found the body," Helen said, turning toward Sloan.

Sloan tried to shift her mind from the memory and focus on the process, which would hopefully lead them to Pete's killer. "I came back because I was concerned about the guys getting…carried away."

Helen's eyebrows climbed into her hairline. "Slugging it out over you?"

Sloan felt heat rise along her neck. "Something like that."

"When you got here the door was open?" Courtney asked.

"Not open," Sloan said. "I had to open the door, but there wasn't a lock, so getting in wasn't a problem."

"Was it dark?" Helen asked.

"Yeah." Sloan thought back to when she'd walked inside. The blackened stillness, the concern she'd had for Aidan, which grew when she'd called out and no one had answered. "I switched on the flashlight on my key ring. Then I spotted the lamp sitting on the sawhorse. I flipped it on, and there was Pete. Dead."

Aidan grabbed her hand and pulled her to his side, and she gratefully leaned on him.

The other two women looked at each other, then Helen suggested they go through, like a play at the local theatre, the actual motions of how different scenarios might go.

Was the position of the body significant? Was the choice of weapon a big clue? Was the proximity of the equipment important? Was the location, Aidan's house, something to consider?

To Sloan the most significant detail was the idea that somebody had been so fiercely furious at Pete that he or she had stabbed him with enough force to kill in that very first blow.

It was chilling.

After Courtney and Helen promised to update the rest of the task force the next day, they left, and Aidan turned to look at Sloan with concerned eyes.

He held her hand. "Are you okay?"

She tried to smile. "No." She twisted his hand and kissed his palm. "But I'm starved."

He drew her against him. "Let's set this aside and enjoy each other."

"Here, here."

With little effort, she lost herself in watching Aidan light the grill, laughing at his intensity over the timing of cooking the steaks. She enjoyed her wine and realized how lucky she was to have friends, family and an amazing man in her life. Pete, for all his easygoing charm, had led an odd, chaotic life. Maybe he enjoyed the mystery and unexpected moments— like jealous husbands shoving him—but she longed for a more settled existence.

She didn't solve mysteries for the excitement, after all. She solved them to bring closure. As goofy as it may seem, she wanted to make a difference in her world and community. Her dad's influence played a role there. As well as the lack of time her mother had had to live out her dreams.

Through all the questions, answers and guessing, she worried about and longed for Aidan. She knew his grief ruled his life. She suspected she'd become his solace, as he'd become a catalyst to her realizing she'd healed her heart after Davis.

In the short term that gave them an excuse to lose themselves in sighs and moans and pleasure. Where that left them in the long term, she had no idea.

At the kitchen table, the cream tapers burning low, she sat back in her chair with a satisfied sigh. "If you get bored with renovating, you could always open a restaurant."

"How do you think Mabel would take that?"

"Probably not well. She's ruled the Palmer's Island culinary world for a long time."

"Having experienced her Friday-night Low Country Boil Extravaganza, I don't think I'd measure up anyway."

Pleasantly stuffed, Sloan smiled. "Mabel does know her local seafood and traditional Southern dishes, but we don't have a steak house. I'm nominating you."

"The mega-grill helped."

"Stop being modest." Her gaze flicked to his, and the relaxed atmosphere cranked up several degrees. She rose and rounded the table. Bracing one hand on his shoulder, she leaned over him, stopping her lips inches from touching his. "I think you're amazing."

He tumbled her into his lap. "You, too, Nancy Drew."

As his lips met hers, she felt the grief drain from her. There was hope and passion and promise in his touch.

There'd been few moments that day when she hadn't thought about him—his body, his scent, the passion in his eyes, the way he made her feel.

As his lips trailed a hot, arousing path down her throat, she arranged her legs on either side of him, closing her eyes in bliss as his hardness was cupped between her thighs. Getting accustomed to him, to their passion probably wasn't wise, but she could certainly fully enjoy it, while she had him in her grasp.

Within seconds, they were stripping off their clothes.

Naked, aroused and impatient, Sloan sat on the kitchen table and drew him between her legs.

"Upstairs," he murmured against her lips.

She wrapped her hand around his erection. "Here."

"The condoms are upstairs." He brought her arms around his neck and pulled her off the table, carrying her from the room. "I guess I need to keep a stash in the utility drawer."

"You certainly do."

"How are you going to explain that to Sister Mary Katherine?"

"I'm not explaining anything. It's your house."

He was laughing as he walked into his bedroom.

Laying her on his bed, he propped himself on his side and stroked his hand down her front, from shoulder to thigh, then back again. "Do we have to be in such a big hurry?"

She arched her back as his fingertips brushed her nipple. "Yes."

He didn't answer with words, but kissed her, long and slow and deep. What was once wild and rushed turned tender. Sloan was less comfortable with that pace. Tender meant emotional, and she was leery of caring too deeply for this volatile man.

Closing her eyes, she concentrated on the arousing sensations each flick of his finger, caress of his tongue or brush of his hand brought on her body. She sighed when he cupped her breast; her breath caught when he slid his hand through the heat between her legs.

He brought her to the brink of sweet release, then shifted and glided his fingers down her arm, her leg, her cheek, making every part of her ache to have him inside her and yet wanting the delicious and sensual torture to go on forever.

When he did enter her, he moved with aching slowness,

inch by inch. She gripped his hips and pushed toward him, craving deeper penetration.

His control was amazing. And frustrating.

This was the master seducer, the player Davis was so eager to warn her about. A man who played with women's bodies as easily and skillfully as he made money. But Sloan could understand why a woman wouldn't care how many he satisfied—as long as she was one of the ones he chose.

As much as she liked to be in control, the vulnerability was alarming.

Yet she trusted him. For reasons she couldn't explain. For reasons she didn't want to acknowledge.

By the time her orgasm shimmered through her, racing up her spine and spreading to every inch of her, she was the one ready to compose poems in his honor. And the worry that her heart was working its way into this arrangement was a distant memory.

As he lay sprawled across her, she stroked his back. "Clearly your talents don't only lie in the culinary world."

Expelling a satisfied sigh, he slid his hand across her stomach. "Maybe I should open a brothel instead of a restaurant."

He'd have a hundred women lined up by noon. Shaking aside the stab of jealousy, she said, "The sheriff would *love* that."

"Then again, maybe not. Your dad is not somebody I want to get on the wrong side of."

"You're a smart guy."

He said nothing for a few minutes, and the ceiling fan overhead spun a light breeze over their skin. "Where's your mother?"

She trailed her fingers through his silky hair. "She died of cancer about a month before I turned two. I barely remember her."

"Your dad never remarried?"

"No. She was the one for him, and I guess he felt he could never replace her. As I got older, I understood how much we looked alike, and I think he's happy seeing her in me."

"Is that why you work so hard for the town?"

"No, that's all him. Part of the code and sense of responsibility he lives by. It seems pretty rare these days—or so people who don't live here tell me."

"So he's never dated in all these years? Doesn't he get lonely?"

"No." She paused, frowning. "Though there's a rumor that he and Mabel—who lost her husband many years ago in a highway accident—have an *arrangement*. I try not to think about it."

He raised his head, his gaze meeting hers. "See, if you had a brothel in town…"

"Oh, very cute. Be sure and use that in your pitch to the business licensing board."

"Is your dad on the board?"

"Of course. Though my granddaddy is the chairman."

"I thought he was a judge. He manages a lot between trials."

"We don't have many trials. If there's a dispute, the sheriff shows up and negotiates the peace. People rarely argue with his solutions and compromises."

"I bet."

She laid her hand alongside his jaw. "Tell me about your parents."

10

AIDAN CURLED his hand into a fist. "It's not really something I discuss."

"Don't turn away," Sloan said, catching his cheek before he could move. "I want to know what happened to them."

"They died."

"They were murdered."

His heart hammering, he backed off the bed. He searched frantically for his jeans. His nakedness was no longer just physical, and he didn't like the sensation at all. "You want some water?" he asked as he jerked on his pants.

She propped herself on her elbows. "No, I'm—"

He spun and headed out of the room.

What's she doing? What's she asking?

Stalking into the kitchen, he grew angrier with every step. They were having sex. They were having fun having sex. He liked her company; he enjoyed getting her feedback on the renovations.

But they weren't a couple. She didn't have the right to poke into his personal business this way. Nobody did. His parents, what happened to them, was private.

He snatched a bottle of water from the fridge and gulped it down. And what good would it do to talk about them anyway?

It was over. They were dead, and nobody would ever pay.

As the rage of that knowledge crashed over him, he sank to the floor, his back propped against the refrigerator door. He'd messed up everything. He hadn't protected them; he hadn't even found them justice.

He'd failed.

Everything in his life had been a glowing success, except for the one thing that mattered—protecting and cherishing his family.

He'd taken them for granted and hadn't appreciated the simple, precious gift they were. Though he'd worked hard at his job, he'd thought he was entitled to a good, easy life. It never occurred to him that something bad would happen. Bad things happened to other people.

Maybe it was his rigid upbringing, or maybe it was some kind of crazy arrogance, but he truly believed that if he'd been a better person, a more thoughtful and caring son, his parents wouldn't have died.

He'd come to Palmer's Island to atone for his mistakes, to remind himself that he was alone in the world because he'd been thoughtless and selfish. He'd wanted to pound nails and sweat and drive himself to exhaustion, so that maybe he could sleep and not wonder if his mother had called for him with her last breath.

He'd come to embrace darkness.

But Sloan wouldn't let him wallow. Her smile and her friends and her committees surrounded him. Suffocating.

At least they should be suffocating.

Instead, the task force, nerdy Penelope, meddling Betsy and Patsy, even Sister Mary Katherine had somehow become a comfort. They offered him the support he didn't deserve.

Wrapped in his robe, Sloan appeared in the doorway. "Do you want me to go?"

He closed his eyes, trying desperately to block out the light she offered. But it was no good. "Please don't."

She sank down beside him and pulled him into her arms.

Swallowing his pain, he laid his head against her breast and let her soothe him.

In the months since he'd lost his parents, he'd never let anyone do that simple thing. Ridiculously simple. Easily done. Yet he hadn't allowed anybody close enough to see his guilt and overwhelming grief.

"They died because of my selfishness," he said finally.

"How so?" she asked, her grip tightening around his waist.

"Everybody knows parts of downtown Atlanta are dangerous, but I insisted on meeting my parents at this particular restaurant. Nothing had ever happened to me. Nothing could. I was rich, smart and successful. I couldn't be touched.

"I didn't send a car for them. I didn't pick them up myself. Even worse, I was so busy finalizing a deal, I was late meeting them. I found them two blocks from the restaurant, their blood on the sidewalk as two strangers gave them CPR."

She rocked him. "I'm so sorry."

"I didn't even know CPR. I couldn't help. I just stood there, watching the life drain out of them."

Sloan said nothing, just kissed his temple.

They held each other in silence for a long while, then he finally found the strength to look at her. She knew his deepest secret now; she knew what a thoughtless ass he could be. She, who rallied her entire community with a snap of her fingers, and over the simplest cause, would never respect him in light of the mistakes he'd made.

To his surprise, tears glimmered in her eyes. "You're not to blame for anything." When he started to interrupt, she laid her finger over his lips. "Maybe you were thoughtless, maybe you didn't appreciate your parents as you should have. That's regret. Not blame. *Everybody* who's lost someone suddenly feels that way."

"But, I—"

"Your situation is extreme. No germ or cell or random crash took your parents from you. Another human being did. It's tough. It sucks."

His pulse pounded. Would the anger ever abate? "I want to crush him into dust."

"Me, too." She stroked his cheek. "Give yourself a break. Take time to heal."

"Why haven't you asked me if the wild media stories were true? The ones about drug deals gone bad? Or me owing money to the mob?"

"I don't care."

He swallowed hard, and something inside him that had been dying before he met her flickered to life again. "Have I mentioned you're amazing?"

"I think so. Come to the oyster roast with me this weekend."

"I—" He angled his head. "The what?"

"The oyster roast." She rose and extended her hand, helping him to his feet. "It's a time-honored, beachside tradition. We raise money for local charities, eat ourselves silly, drink some beer and dance like idiots."

The guilt and blame weren't gone, even through her comfort and obvious distractions. Maybe they never would be.

Maybe they weren't supposed to.

But he was glad he'd let her see him, all of him, and he was even happier she'd seen the worst and was sticking around.

He squeezed her hand. "If you're wearing a bikini, I'm all for roasting anything you like."

"So, ARE YOU going to tell me about the naughty affair you're having with superhottie Aidan Kendrick?"

Sitting in the salon chair, her hair glimmering with foil packets, Sloan met Courtney's gaze in the mirror. "No."

"Come *on.*" Courtney waved her brush, covered with creamy hair color. "Give a single-and-looking gal some juicy details to keep hope alive."

Sloan twisted around to stare at Courtney in disbelief. "You hear more juicy confessions than Father Dominick."

Courtney grabbed another piece of foil and slid it against Sloan's roots. "Mostly they exaggerate."

"Do they?"

"Sure. So the least you could do is make something up."

Sloan grinned. "I don't have to."

Courtney groaned. "You're a terrible tease."

"Sorry, I'm just not ready to share."

"Oh." Courtney painted color on another section of hair. "Does he feel the same?"

"How?"

"All fluttery and twitchy."

"I seriously doubt he feels fluttery and twitchy." She narrowed her eyes. "Neither do I, for the record."

"I guess you could be classified as more twisty than twitchy."

"I'm not twisty or twitchy," Sloan said heatedly.

"Then you might want to let go of my poncho."

Sloan glanced at her lap, annoyed and amazed to realize she was twisting the vinyl poncho, designed to protect her clothes from being stained by the hair color, in knots.

So maybe Aidan's confessions about his parents' deaths had her a little tense. While she was glad he'd unloaded the burdens he'd been carrying for so long, and she was sure it would help his grieving process, casual lovers didn't share that kind of moment.

Would this change their relationship? If so, was that necessarily a bad thing? Maybe this would bond them as friends, so that when they went their separate ways, they could do so amicably.

And that was crap.

If he calmly, and in a friendly way, told her he was attracted to somebody else and wanted to end things with her—exactly as her last lover had—somebody was going to get hurt. Seriously, physically hurt, not just boo-hooey tears.

"You sure you don't want to share?" Courtney asked as she set the timer for the color.

"No." Sloan made an effort to relax her hands. "So, what did Betsy and Patsy have to say about Pete's case?"

"They seemed to think that a woman as a killer was unlikely, due to the strength of that first blow."

"So the jealous-husband theory lives on?"

"Do you have something different?"

"No." Sloan shook her head. "I don't know. I need to talk to my dad."

"Not a bad idea. He was by here earlier for his monthly trim, then he was heading back out to the crime scene."

"The—" Sloan, completely unconcerned about her hair sticking out in all directions and wrapped in foil, jolted from her chair. "He's going to see Aidan."

Courtney laid her hand on Sloan's shoulder and pushed her back down. "Chill, girl. He's not going over there to arrest him."

"But he'll know. He always knows."

"You mean about you and the sexy homeowner getting horizontal?"

"Of course. Things didn't exactly go well with him and my last boyfriend."

"I doubt Davis still holds that night in jail against you. The sheriff does tend to take matters into his own hands."

Sloan felt the urge to crawl under Courtney's stylist station. "And look how that relationship worked out."

"So you'd classify Aidan Kendrick as your *boyfriend?*"

"Oh, good grief. Would you clamp down on the gossip gene for a minute?" Sloan tried to stand again, only to have Courtney try to force her down. "I'm having a crisis."

"And if you run out of here looking like that you'll never forgive me or yourself, plus there's always the chance that some smart-ass blogger will take a picture of you and post it to the Web. Plus the bleach will fry your hair until it turns blue."

Sloan sat.

She waited out the timer, all the while envisioning Aidan thrown in jail or otherwise intimidated by her dad.

When four minutes were left, the bell over the front door to Courtney's shop jingled. An attractive, tanned, fit-looking woman walked inside. She wore a crisp white tennis dress, and her dark hair was pulled high into a ponytail.

"Well, look what we have here," Courtney said in a quiet voice.

"What?" She nodded discreetly toward the brunette. "Who is she?"

"Marla Hanson."

Sloan took a longer, more suspicious look at the woman, whose biceps and forearms looked plenty strong enough to wield more than a tennis racket with serious strength. "How interesting."

Between the library, the historical society fund-raisers or her connection to the sheriff, nearly everybody in town knew who Sloan was. But she didn't necessarily know all of them, and she'd never met Marla Hanson.

At least not yet.

"Introduce me," she said to Courtney.

"How am I supposed to do that?" Courtney whispered back. "Hey, Marla, this is Sloan Caldwell, you know, the *sheriff's* daughter. She was wondering if your knife skills are as good as your backhand?"

"You might try something slightly more discreet." Sloan smiled slyly. "I wouldn't want to scare away my best suspect."

"Suspect? I thought we agreed it was a jealous boyfriend."

"That's Betsy and Patsy's theory."

"Come on, Sloan. Marla's a client. I can't afford to go losing good customers."

"Don't you want to know if one of your customers is a homicidal maniac?"

"As long as she doesn't get homicidal in here, no."

Sloan knew that statement was all bluster. Courtney was as concerned about who had killed Pete—and why—as she was. The murder had draped a pall over the town. People had been coming into the library all morning dressed in unusually somber clothes, and since everybody now seemed to know she'd found the body, asking whispered questions.

"I never should have told you about the shoving match between Pete and Marla's husband," Courtney said grumpily.

"Why did you?"

"I'm genetically incapable of not passing on hot information. My grandmother was the same way."

The timer went off, so Courtney got busy rinsing and washing the color from Sloan's hair. In hurried murmurs, they decided that Courtney would casually walk Sloan to the door—right beside the stylist who was working on Marla. Then she'd—again *casually*—mention the tragedy about Pete.

With her hair lightened, blown-dry and styled, Sloan followed Courtney across the shop. Courtney stopped to speak to two stylists before approaching Marla's. "Hey, Erin," she said. "How're things going?"

"Good. Marla's thinking about highlights. Red tones or caramel?"

This is perfect, Sloan thought. *Very casual.*

Courtney's gaze roved Marla's face. "Caramel, definitely."

"That's what I thought, too," Erin said.

"Sloan, do you know Erin and Marla?" Courtney asked, turning to her.

"Erin and I have met," she said.

"Oh, well, Marla Henson, this is Sloan Caldwell. You know, the sheriff's daughter."

Sloan resisted the urge to give Courtney a sharp look, and shook Marla's hand. "Nice to meet you."

Marla's light brown gaze met Sloan's briefly. "You, too."

"Isn't this business with Pete Willis just horrible?"

"Oh, my gosh, yes," Erin said. "Marla and I were just talking about him. Pete built a deck at the Hansons' last summer."

"How terrible." Courtney paused. "Well, I don't mean his work was terrible. Actually, I've heard he was a really good carpenter. I just mean how terrible that you knew him and everything. Were you really close?"

This time Sloan couldn't resist. She glared at Courtney and hoped the hairdresser's babbling speech hadn't ruined their hopes of getting information. "I'm sure Marla isn't interested in gossiping about Pete, even if they were close."

Despite her new partner's lousy interrogating skills, Sloan

knew what she was doing. The best way to get people to talk was not to ask any questions at all.

And it was certainly true for Marla.

"Oh, we weren't close," she said with a dismissive flip of her manicured hand. "My husband actually hired him. I spend most of my summers on the court. He did a decent job with the deck, though my husband said he'd expected better." She shrugged. "Looks fine to me."

"He was working out at Batherton Mansion when he was killed, wasn't he?" Erin shuddered. "That place always gave me the creeps. That rich business guy from Atlanta better *really* be loaded. He'll never get rid of the place now."

"Helen thinks this will make it famous," Courtney said.

"Really?" Erin grinned. "After you solve this case, is that going to be your next historical committee fund-raiser, Sloan? Tours of the now-haunted house?"

Well, hell.

Then again, maybe Marla wouldn't notice that she was in the presence of an amateur detective.

"Oh, that's right." Marla's eyes grew speculative. "I read about you in the newspaper a couple of times. You help your dad solve his cases."

"Not really," Sloan said. "The paper exaggerates."

"That's *so* right, isn't it?" Courtney said, gesturing dramatically. "Just because she caught that burglar that time. And recovered Mrs. Anderson's ruby necklace. I think it was the gardener who'd helped himself to her jewelry case. Anyway, *please,* it was all blind luck on Sloan's part."

Sloan wanted to stomp on her friend's foot. Or tape her mouth. *Way* too much information. She needed to get moving before Courtney told Marla she was on the freakin' suspect

list. "It certainly was," Sloan agreed. "I need to get back to
the library. I'll see you ladies later. Courtney, I still need to
pay you, don't I?"

If Courtney hadn't realized she'd bungled the questioning,
she certainly took hints well. "Absolutely. I've got to charge
even my friends to keep us all beautiful."

At the counter, Sloan handed over her credit card and whispered to Courtney, "If she did do it, she's a pretty cool killer.
She didn't so much as blink when you said *sheriff*."

"She was *too* cool, if you ask me. And aren't her eyes
beady? They looked pretty beady to me."

"Don't go applying for your P.I. license just yet, Sam
Spade."

Courtney waved her hand. "No, no. Not Sam Spade. Didn't
Nancy Drew have girlfriends that helped with her cases?"

"Bess and George."

"George?"

"I think it stood for Georgia. Or maybe Georgette."

"Still, I'll be Bess. Helen can be George."

"Now that we have the important information out of the
way," Sloan said, leaning on the counter and the sarcasm.
"What did you think about her denial of knowing Pete, of
barely noticing him even?"

"Very suspicious. And it goes completely against what
Erin said about her bragging about Pete *and* the pushing
match between Pete and her husband."

"Later, after Marla leaves, get with Erin and find out more
details." Sloan slipped on her sunglasses. "I've got to go stop
my boyfriend from possibly being dragged off to jail."

Courtney's face broke in a wide smile. "So he *is* your boyfriend!"

"YOU'RE ALL SET," Penelope announced.

In his library, arranging books on the shelves, Aidan looked over to where the teenager sat at his desk. "Already?"

"Setting up a computer is pretty much a color-coded system now." She smiled. "I bet even *you* could have handled it."

Sister Mary Katherine, sitting on the other side of the desk and knitting, didn't look up, but cleared her throat loudly. "Mr. Kendrick is your employer. We don't give our employers cheeky answers to professional questions."

"Of course, Sister," Penelope said. She stood, faced Aidan and rolled her shoulders. "Mr. Kendrick, the laptop system you hired me to set up through my school's new community program, Teens in Business, is operational and ready for use."

"Thank you, Miss Penelope. I appreciate your dedication to the project, as well as the swiftness with which you completed it."

They both glanced at the sister, who nodded and continued knitting.

With the business of satisfying the chaperone out of the way, Aidan and Penelope got down to the serious business of loading the games he'd bought onto the computer. They were well into a sound-muted match of Diner Dash when the doorbell rang.

"Why don't you try the next antique shop's Web site on the list?" Aidan suggested to Penelope with a wink. "I'll get the door."

His easy attitude vanished when he saw the sheriff on his porch. "Sheriff," he said with a brief nod.

"You can call me Buddy, remember?"

Aidan let his gaze rake the sheriff from the top of his brown Stetson to the tips of his snakeskin boots. Buddy just didn't work for him. "No, I really don't think I can."

The sheriff chuckled. "Mind if I come in?"

Aidan stepped back and invited him inside. "I was in the library, doing some computer work." He walked that way, and the sheriff followed. "I assume you know Penelope and Sister Mary Katherine?"

Taking off his hat, Buddy nodded at both ladies, then his gaze centered on Penelope. "It's barely after one o'clock. Am I gonna have to arrest you for truancy?"

The nun gave him a stern look. "Penelope is part of the school's working-in-the-community program, Sheriff. She receives school credit, as well as job experience for her efforts. Never fear, the Order has her education well in hand."

The sheriff nodded. "Of course, Sister. Your school is one of the finest in the state."

Aidan had no idea if the sheriff had come to talk about Sloan, or Pete's case, but neither seemed appropriate for the women in the room. "Do you need to talk to me privately?" he asked the other man. "We can go in the kitchen."

"Sure."

As the sheriff sauntered down the hall, Aidan turned toward Penelope. "Why don't you start a spreadsheet where I can keep track of furniture and accessories? I need to know which ones I have, which ones I've bought and which ones I need."

"I'm on it, bos—" She stopped, glancing at the nun. "Yes, sir, Mr. Kendrick."

"I've got a pot of coffee going," Aidan said when he entered the kitchen. "You want some?"

The sheriff folded his large body into a kitchen chair. "I can always drink coffee."

Aidan poured two mugs, handing one to the sheriff. They sipped in silence for a moment, then the other man commented, "Nice and strong. Kinda has a different flavor, too."

"It's a Costa Rican reserve blend."

The sheriff paused with his mug in the air. "Are you talkin' whiskey or coffee?"

"It's coffee. Just the fancy kind."

"You really are a sophisticated city boy, aren't you?"

"I guess I am." Aidan rested a hip against the counter. "Or I was."

"Mostly I don't care for sophisticated city boys. The last time my girl took up with one of 'em I spent a lot of time bitin' my tongue." He grinned. "Well, except that time I locked him in jail. Anyways, I mostly kept quiet, and he predictably broke her heart. I always regretted it."

"Keeping quiet or locking him in jail?"

The sheriff toasted him with his mug. "See, I like you." He shook his head. "Not sure why, except maybe that smart tone reminds me of my Sloan. Her mama always had a way with words, too."

"Did Davis really break Sloan's heart?"

"Ah-ha. I thought you might jump on that." He angled his head. "I think so. Leastways, I was sure until you came along. But she didn't seem too concerned about him Saturday night. She seemed much more interested in you."

"Good to know, since I'm very much interested in her."

"Which is why you're also interested in Davis Curnan."

"Definitely. Do you mind? I knew him professionally when he worked for me, but not personally. He and Sloan don't seem to fit, and I'm trying to understand what made them a couple."

"I don't mind. Long as you don't mind getting locked in jail if you make her cry."

"I can live with that." He sipped coffee. "Why do you call Davis a city boy? I thought he grew up here."

"He did, but Palmer's Island was never good enough for

him. He always thought he was smarter. He had bigger and better plans for places he'd go and bigger, better ideas for how to do things."

"Yeah, I know about that. He must have sent me a hundred e-mails over six months, always claiming to have a superior system."

"Annoying as the devil."

Aidan nodded. "No kidding. But not annoying to Sloan apparently."

"He was kind of nerdy—and acted too much like a know-it-all—when they were in high school, and she had plenty of dates, but she eventually got bored with all of them. She ran into Davis at a town fund-raiser. He'd grown up some, but he was still smart. She liked that. So they started goin' out. He was always takin' her to nice places, doing nice things for her. He respected her opinions and really listened to her when she talked." He glanced at Aidan. "Women like that stuff."

"So I hear."

"But then he up and moved to Atlanta. They tried to keep things going, but it didn't last long. He found somebody else, and she cried a lot."

"So you tossed him in jail."

"Nah." He paused, smiling slightly. "Well, yeah. I *did* put him in jail, but that was way before they broke up. He and some of his buddies had a poker night, drank too much. They decided to walk home, but they were weavin' into traffic on Church Street, so I hauled 'em in. Really for their own protection.

"In the mornin' I gave them the standard speech about moderation, or, at the very least, somebody staying sober enough either to drive or take care of everybody else. Davis got smart with me, saying how I exaggerated them weaving along the street. Pissed me off."

"And Sloan took his side?"

"No. She trusted me more than him."

"Which pissed him off."

"Probably so."

The picture the sheriff painted explained a lot. Sloan, confident and sexy, had her pick of men, and she'd picked the one who impressed her the most, who treated her the best.

But something had clearly been missing.

"So I reckon you're planning on staying?" the sheriff asked.

Last night, the grief and anger he'd shared with Sloan had been intense. Part of him wanted to run from their bond. Part of him wanted to be embarrassed by his vulnerability. Part of him wanted to hang on to her with both hands. Part of him was afraid to want her too much. And part of him was worried he was relying on her too much and not standing on his own.

One thing was for certain—he had too many damn parts.

"The renovations will take several months," he said vaguely.

"You'd better be more certain with Sloan."

"With all due respect, sir, we're happy with how things are."

"Uh-huh. And what happens when somebody *isn't* happy?"

Aidan said nothing for a long moment, then confessed, "I have no idea."

"Women—and especially Sloan—for all their independence, want commitment. They want to know you're going to be there with them through all the fun, and the not-so-fun."

"Sloan and I have already had not-so-fun."

"Yeah." His gaze met Aidan's. "I expect Pete's death brought back some bad memories for you."

Aidan nodded. He didn't want to go into his history. "We were talking about Sloan. She's always had you to count on."

"And she always will. That doesn't mean she doesn't want

more." He cleared his throat. "Truthfully, I think her high expectations come from me. Her mama and I were a team, and even though she was only little when Rosaline died, I told Sloan about her all the time. I wanted her to know she came from love—a great love." He stopped and seemed unwilling, or unable, to continue.

"My parents had the same thing."

"Sloan wants what I had. What, I'm guessing, your parents had. She won't settle for less."

"I don't know what I want."

"That's a problem." The sheriff held up his hand. "Maybe not now. But its somethin' to think about."

"I'm considering everything."

The sheriff nodded. "I hope you are."

Aidan stewed on his words for a few minutes, but knew the sheriff had other things on his mind besides his daughter's romance with the new guy in town. "Have there been any new developments with Pete's case?"

The sheriff switched topics with ease. "I spent Sunday at his apartment, searching for anything that might lead us to his killer, but got nothin'. I've subpoenaed his financial records, but the bank manager says Pete was responsible, but didn't have a lot of money. He can't imagine anybody wantin' to kill him for it. I have to wait for the official records. But I tend to trust the bank guy."

"Pete may not have money, but I do. Maybe somebody intended to rob me."

"Could be. But I don't think so. Your average B-and-E man doesn't carry a knife. Too confrontational, too messy." The sheriff waved his hand dismissively. "A knife is personal, so Pete's issues were personal, not financial. No random guy, no matter what the paper might print, walked in here and stabbed Pete to death. At least that's what the SLED investigator and I are figuring on."

"SLED?"

"South Carolina Law Enforcement Division. They help out all the law-enforcement agencies in the state. They've got way more resources and experience with this kind of thing. Anyway, I'm copying this investigator on all my findings. He said he'll come down if we need more manpower or anything."

"Might be good to have—" The sound of someone pounding on the front door interrupted him. Before he could begin to wonder who that could be, he heard a familiar voice shout "Daddy!"

The sheriff smiled, then calmly sipped his coffee. "That's my quiet, demure Southern belle."

11

SLOAN BARGED into the kitchen. "Leave him—"

She ground to a halt as she noticed Aidan standing by the counter and her dad sitting at the table. Both held coffee mugs and looked at her with expressions ranging from amusement on her dad's part to confusion on Aidan's.

"Somethin' wrong, pumpkin?" her dad asked.

"What are you doing here?" she demanded, planting her hands on her hips.

"Having coffee, talking about Pete. Do I get a kiss?"

With a sigh, she walked over to him and brushed her lips across his cheek.

"Don't I get one, too?" Aidan asked.

Noting his teasing smile, she figured her dad hadn't been torturing him. At least not yet. She crossed to him and gave him a chaste peck on the cheek. "You seem fine."

"Why wouldn't I be?"

Sister Mary Katherine, out of breath, appeared in the doorway, a curious Penelope peering over her shoulder. "Is something wrong? Sloan, are you all right?"

Embarrassed, Sloan pressed her lips together. *Overreact much, Sloan?* "Everything's fine. I just…"

"She was worried I was intimidating and torturing her new boyfriend," the sheriff said.

Sloan winced at the word *boyfriend.* Aidan would probably love that description.

To her surprise, he turned his head and stared at her. "I don't intimidate too easily."

She searched his gaze. What did that mean? Was he her boyfriend? Did she want him to be her boyfriend? This whole thing was moving pretty fast from where she stood, and she wasn't really sure—

"Good heavens, child," Sister Mary Katherine said, her tone slightly reproving. "You nearly gave me a heart attack."

The sheriff immediately rose and guided the sister to a chair at the table. Penelope took a seat, as well. And Aidan frowned.

Here he was, surrounded by her clan of friends. Were they getting on his nerves, or was he starting to get used to them?

"Aren't you supposed to be at the library?" he asked her.

Okay. So maybe it was her he was frowning at. Romance was so damn confusing and complicated sometimes.

"I called the volunteer and asked her to stay a bit longer. I needed to talk to Daddy about Pete's case." She faced her dad. "Are there any new developments?"

"Nothing much," he said vaguely.

"Maybe I can help," she said. "I could check out his apartment."

"I already went to the apartment. There's nothing there that explains why he was killed."

"Did you check out the computer?"

"Sure."

Sloan narrowed her eyes. Her dad was notoriously leery of computers. He knew how to turn them on and not much else.

"I'm gonna have the guy from the computer store go over it later in the week," he added defensively.

"Why wait 'til then?" Sloan asked. "We have a computer expert right here."

The sheriff's gaze slid to Penelope. He lowered his voice. "I'm not taking a teenager to a dead man's apartment."

Sloan leaned forward. "It's not like the dead man will be there. I went to plenty of crime scenes when I was a teenager."

"You were different, and you never went to the scene of a violent crime."

Sister Mary Katherine rose. "If you'd like Penelope's help with a computer, Sheriff, I have no objections. There's nothing more important to the community right now than finding who took that poor boy's life."

Penelope nodded. "I want to help."

The sheriff glanced at Aidan.

"Sorry, Sheriff," Aidan said. "I have to side with the ladies on this one. And, to be technical, Penelope is closer to the crime scene right now."

The sheriff grunted his acknowledgement. "It's creepy."

"I know, Daddy," Sloan said, stroking her father's arm, her tone conciliatory. "But we'll be there with her. You could even get the computer and bring it back here, if that will make you feel better."

"Too many wires," he said gruffly, though his face had softened like butter. "Wouldn't know what to unplug first."

"Fine, then." Sloan smiled. "We'll meet back here at five-thirty and head over to Pete's together. Is that convenient for everybody?"

When all of them agreed, she kissed her father's cheek again, then started down the hall. "You want to walk me to my car, Aidan?" she asked, turning back briefly. "I have something for you."

"Right behind you," he said, setting aside his mug.

As they stepped out onto the porch, she turned toward him, looped her arms around his neck and fused her lips with his.

He held her tight around the waist, and she absorbed the feel and scent of him, the zing in her blood as she slid her tongue into his mouth, the way he responded by lightly sinking in his teeth. She jerked back and slapped her hand on his chest, then he grinned and pulled her close again, gentling his touch, caressing her…seemingly inside and out.

Parting, they were both out of breath. And the moment seemed heavier than it should. He brushed his finger down her cheek, then kissed her there. The tenderness conflicted with her pounding pulse. With the emotions coursing through her.

The ones that wanted her to cling to him, depend on him… love him.

Her heart jumped against her chest. Could she? Was she?

He leaned his forehead against hers, then pressed his lips to hers again briefly. "You do know how to get the heat going."

She bumped her hips against his. "Where, exactly, did that heat go?"

"All to one spot. Can I show you later?"

"You bet."

"How about I actually take you out to dinner?"

She raised her eyebrows. "There's not a big selection in Palmer's Island, but there's one or two nice places."

"So I hear. I have an assistant who's an island specialist."

"Penelope's your assistant now?"

"She's smart, efficient, competent and sassy—at least when the good sister isn't within hearing distance." He cocked his head. "Like somebody else I know."

"She's a talented girl." Sloan smiled knowingly. "So if Penelope is on restaurant reservation duty, I'll bet we're going to the Lighthouse."

His bright expression fell. "She told you."

"No. She's been hoping Jimmy Malone will ask her out and take her there for nearly six months." She poked him in the ribs. "So, I'm wearing a short, hot dress and heels?"

The fire in his eyes said everything. "I certainly hope so."

"Mmm. Okay." She pressed her lips to his briefly. Dear heaven, he tasted fabulous. "Then think…red."

Carefully, she reached into her bag, pulled out a folded slip of paper and handed it to him.

He opened it and read aloud "'Check out Marla Hanson.'" He glanced at her. "What's this?"

"The something I brought for you that you can tell my dad about." She grinned as she turned and strode toward her sleek, black convertible sports car. "Believe me, he'll ask."

Though Aidan walked around Pete's with some of the other members of the task force, they found nothing very significant.

Penelope searched through the computer files and ran across client billing statements, supply lists, instructions for staining crown molding…and then a racy e-mail, at which point Sloan took over reading, finding several more. The messages were from two different senders, but the addresses gave them no clue to the authors. Penelope spent some time tracking down the origins, but couldn't pull out a legitimate name.

They helped the sheriff pack up the computer so it could be delivered to the local computer store in hopes that something significant would be found.

Sister Mary Katherine brought a box to gather some of Pete's personal things, which she promised to send to his family in California. The clothes, furniture and electronics, at the family's direction, were to be given to the church, so they could either sell them or donate them to people in need.

As they left the apartment, Aidan couldn't help wondering what the sister would pack up from his house if something happened to him.

Nothing.

Everything would be sold or donated. He had no family anymore. His parents had both been only children, as was he. His grandparents had long since passed away.

He thought of the box of his parents' personal items that had been delivered by the service he'd hired to clean out their house. Too angry, he hadn't even bothered to go through their things himself. *Just pay somebody to do it, and don't get involved. Don't let the emotional damage of what's happened affect you.* That had been his rationalization.

It had done him no good.

Instead, the rage and helplessness of not being able to change what had happened, not being able even to punish the one responsible, had built. Built and churned and bubbled inside until it had finally exploded all over Sloan.

What would he do without her?

He shook his head and climbed into the car beside her. Thinking that way about a woman he'd known a little over a week was crazy.

But still, the craziness continued.

After leaving Pete's, she dropped him off at his house, then returned a couple of hours later in a red dress that literally made his jaw drop. The Lighthouse also delivered on its romantic, oceanfront billing. They held hands and watched the sun set as they walked on the beach; they talked as if they'd known each other forever and had all the time in the world.

BEFORE HE KNEW IT, the week had passed, and it was Friday night. The oyster roast was due to start in less than two hours.

Was he thinking back on all he'd accomplished with the house that week? How beautiful the new dining-room table was? Or thinking back over the last several nights he'd spent with Sloan, the hot red dress, the sexy lingerie and the sexy things they'd done on the dining-room table? Or was he even going over Pete's case in his mind for the thousandth time, trying to find a new angle, a possibility none of them had considered?

No.

He, like seemingly everybody else on the island, was in the beachside park preparing for the roast. They were hauling food, setting up grills, tables, chairs, tents and even putting together a stage on the beach for the band. Like apparently everything on the island, the oyster roast was a community project. This project also had the added pressure of being a major fund-raiser.

Benefiting music camps at two local churches, the event was also the sole funds provider for the summer beach patrol, which made sure visitors to the island enjoyed themselves, but followed all the ordinances. The fund-raiser was celebrating its twenty-fifth anniversary, and the people of Palmer's Island intended to make it better than ever.

"What's all the shrimp for?" he asked Courtney as he dragged a cooler full of seafood across the sand toward one of the cooking tents. "I thought this was an oyster roast."

"And Low Country boil."

Even after only living on the island a few weeks, he knew all about that local specialty. A combination of shrimp, sausage, corn and potatoes, which was boiled with special seasonings in a big pot, the dish was an institution in the area.

"Hurry," Courtney said, carrying a box of seasonings. "Chef François will be here any minute."

He also knew about Chef François, who owned the Lighthouse. He was an eccentric, temperamental, but brilliant chef who'd shunned the high-profile restaurants in Charleston and opened his own small place on Palmer's Island. Residents both feared him and were awed by him.

When they reached the tent, Aidan parked his rolling cooler next to what looked like dozens of others and glanced around at the endless boxes, bags, pots and giant spoons that had been unloaded from vans in the parking lot, lugged across the wooden walkway over the dunes, then dragged across the sand. "Are we feeding an army?"

"I hope so." With a tired sigh, Courtney set down her box. "If only we could get this kind of event together for the historical committee."

Aidan wiped sweat from his face with a napkin. "Why can't you?"

"We only maintain two buildings on the island—the first church established and a beach house once owned by a pirate. There's just not enough interest. Or money." She looked at him, her face flushed. "But that's not important tonight. We're supposed to be having fun."

"I'm not having any fun yet."

She linked their arms and led them out of the tent. "You will. Only three more coolers to go."

Since Aidan's goal for the night was to eat himself silly and watch Sloan dance in a skimpy bikini, this wasn't much of a sales pitch. But he went along anyway.

True to Courtney's promise, barely half an hour later Chef François' pots were boiling, his assistants were scrambling to please him, the air was filled with enticing scents and Aidan was taking a break with a bottle of water. Sloan, wearing a skimpy, pink bikini top and a flower-patterned skirt, was walking toward him.

She kissed his cheek when she reached his side. "I see you survived cooler duty."

"Courtney said I have ten minutes before I'm put on speaker-hauling duty. Does she ever slow down?"

"Not that I've seen."

His gaze slid over her, her breasts peeking out of her sparkling bikini, the seeming miles of tanned skin, and his pulse picked up speed. "At least you've given me the strength to carry on."

She laid her hands on his shoulders and leaned into him. "So, later—"

Aidan jumped back as he noticed Sister Mary Katherine treading through the sand toward them.

At least he thought it was the nun.

She was wearing her normal headpiece, but she was dressed in a flowing, bright-yellow shirt and skirt, decorated with palm trees. Both covered her from neck to ankles, but her feet were bare, and the outfit was such a stark contrast from her normal black and white, he was stunned.

"What's the matter, Mr. Kendrick?" she asked when she reached them. "Never seen a nun in a bathing suit before?"

"No," he said slowly. "No, I can't say I have."

Sloan giggled.

The sister planted her hands on her hips. "Back to work, you two. The sheriff just radioed and said cars are already pulling into the parking lot."

Aidan glanced at her hand, which held a walkie-talkie. He'd been so distracted by the rest of her, he hadn't noticed. "Once the ticket-holding public gets here, does that mean we stop working?"

Sloan and the sister looked at him with a mixture of pity and exasperation in their eyes.

"Who do you think is going to serve all those people?" the nun asked.

Aidan didn't need to be told he would be serving; he simply turned around and headed back toward the parking lot.

Still, several exhausting hours later, the sun having long ago disappeared from the sky, he sat in a beach chair beside Sloan. Both of them were full of Chef François' delicious seafood, so Aidan figured the work had been worth it. The band was playing a combination of lively rock and soulful blues to satisfy the kids and the couples. Velma had closed for the night and moved the bar to the beach. Sloan was sipping something fruity and rum-filled; he was enjoying a beer. They'd raised over twenty thousand dollars, so event directors Courtney and the good sister were pleased.

And Aidan realized he was happy. Happy and content for the first time in a long, long while.

He linked his hand with Sloan's. "What are you wearing underneath that skirt?"

She met his gaze, her eyes glittering with desire and amusement. "You'll find out later."

"I like the sound of that. How much later?"

"A-hem."

Aidan looked up—and up—to see the sheriff frowning down at them. "Before you two go anywhere, I'd like a dance with my daughter."

Then you'd better do it fast was Aidan's only thought.

"Sure, Daddy." Sloan let her father help her to her feet, then winked at Aidan over her shoulder. "I'll be back soon."

He'd waited all night to be with her. What was a few more minutes?

Deciding he might as well get another beer while he waited, he headed to the bar. Over there, he spoke to several people who'd done set-up duty with him. Sloan had introduced him simply as Aidan, and he'd enjoyed the anonymity.

On an island as small as the one where they all lived, people had to realize the last name and sensational story that came with it. The strange, sullen ex-communications mogul who lived in an empty house, surrounded by overgrown bushes and hidden from the world.

But nobody gave any indication that they knew, or, if they did, that they cared.

They talked about island happenings, their kids' soccer games or swim meets. Even the subject of Pete seemed to be tabled for the relaxed party atmosphere.

After a few minutes, moving away from crowds and the lighted bar area, he stood in the shadows and watched Sloan glide around the dance floor.

Her skin gleamed beneath the moonlight. Her hips swayed to the beat of the music.

He hardened—a practically normal condition these days. Yet he was in no hurry to ease the ache. And with Sloan he liked the anticipation, knowing he'd have her again, knowing they'd satisfy each other until neither of them could move.

Then he heard his name mentioned by a familiar voice.

"…Aidan is really going to let us do it?" Courtney asked.

He glanced a few feet away to see Courtney and Helen, sipping pink drinks from plastic glasses. They obviously didn't see him.

"I hope so," Helen said urgently. "We *need* his house on that brochure."

"No kidding, but Sloan is head of the historical committee. I suppose it's her call on whether or not to approach him."

"But she said she would talk to him."

"It's only been a few weeks," Courtney retorted, though she sounded worried. "Do you think she can convince him to do it?"

Helen laughed. "Are you kidding? Sloan can get *any* man to do *any*thing."

His pulse pounding, Aidan thought back to earlier in the week, when Sloan had talked her dad into letting Penelope go to Pete's apartment. Clearly, Sloan knew how to get her way with her father. Hell, she got her way with everybody. Aidan had always been comforted by the fact that he wasn't the only one affected by her spell.

But Helen's spin was unsettling.

"I guess she'd better get on with it," Courtney said. "We need something professional and eye-catching to take to cor- porations if we expect to attract a decent sponsor."

"And no rich summer tourists are going to cough up big bucks based on that black-and-white photocopied brochure we have now. We need better advertising, and that house is the key."

Courtney nodded. "Maybe we should call for another com- mittee meeting and remind her about the vote."

Watching them move away, Aidan's head began to throb. A brochure? Corporations and tourists? In *his* house?

Sloan keeping secrets. The entire historical committee keeping secrets. Voting about him?

What the hell was all that about?

He tossed his beer in the trash and moved, unseeing, toward the ocean. Stopping when he reached the edge of the sand, he stared at the crashing and receding waves and tried to con- vince himself he'd heard wrong. That Sloan and her fellow committee members weren't hoping to convince him to let them use his house for a brochure and advertising campaign. And that they'd kept that agenda a secret for the entire time he'd known them.

When Sloan's arms slid around his waist from behind, he stiffened.

"I thought I'd lost you," she said softly.

He closed his eyes against the sound of her voice. What else had she lied about? "When were you planning to tell me about the brochure?"

Her hands clenched against his stomach. "What brochure?"

"The historical society one featuring my house. The one you're supposed to convince me to be a part of."

Letting go, she walked around to face him. "Who told you?"

"I overheard Helen and Courtney talking about it. Is that what you've been doing with me the last two weeks, *convincing* me?"

She tipped her head. "How could I convince you if I haven't even mentioned it?"

"We communicate pretty well without words."

She said nothing for a long moment, then realization seemed to crash over her like the waves. "You're not serious," she said, her tone incredulous. "You think I'm sleeping with you so you'll let us use your house for a brochure?"

"Are you?"

Her eyes flashed with anger. "You are completely out of your mind. Why in the hell would I—" She drew a deep breath and made a visible effort to calm down. "Look, Aidan, I'm sorry you found out that way, but you're making a much bigger deal out of the brochure than it is."

"Helen and Courtney seemed to think it was a big deal. You're running out of time to attract corporate sponsors and summer tourists. Are you planning to offer guided tours? Or maybe that's my job? Should I go ahead and invest in some velvet ropes for my bedroom? This is where the homeowner screws the sheriff's daughter every night."

"Stop it."

But he couldn't. Anger and betrayal were boiling inside him. "Then again, I guess you could have gotten Penelope, or maybe the good sister to keep sending me off on errands, so I wouldn't even be there. Were you planning on telling me at all?"

"I was planning to ask you," she said, her tone just as hard and angry as his. "I wasn't concerned about the tourist season. I was concerned about you. And I didn't ask you at first because I knew you'd never agree, and I haven't mentioned it up till now because I know you don't want to draw attention to yourself. You want to be left alone."

"What I want doesn't seem to matter," he practically shouted at her. "People are filing in and out of there like it's a damn airport."

She blinked, and he knew he'd hurt her. He wasn't sure if he'd intended to or not. He only knew that the hollowness in his stomach, which had been there ever since he'd heard the damn word *brochure,* seemed as if it would never be filled.

"They're around because of me," she said quietly. "My life is full of people. I like it that way. Obviously, you don't."

There'd been many times he'd been irritated by all the people, but lately he didn't mind so much. He didn't exactly like all the activity, but he knew Sloan did, so he accepted them.

But he'd moved to the middle of nowhere for a reason. Somehow, in the last couple of weeks that reason had gotten lost in his lust for her.

"If you want to be alone so badly, Aidan, be my guest."

As she stormed away, he tried to remember his purpose for coming to the island.

He was supposed to be remembering his parents, grieving for them and trying to change his life, trying to make up for all he'd lost. He didn't want anything to do with corporate sponsorships and ad campaigns. And especially not the media. He wanted the house to be beautiful and selfless, two things he definitely wasn't.

But standing alone on the beach, he felt as though he'd lost everything all over again.

12

HOLDING THE PHONE receiver, Sloan listened to the fourth ring and nearly hung up. But she was so hoping somebody would accept her comfort in their time of grief.

Since Aidan the Ass was in no mood.

Did he honestly believe she was spending every night in his bed, feeding him, trying to get him to be part of the community, talking him through his grief and helping him with the house just so she could convince him to be part of the brochure? That she was so desperate for money she planned to bring groups of gawking tourists through his house?

She glared at the churning ocean, just a few hundred yards from her condo's screened deck, as if daring it to agree.

"Hello?"

Thankful to put aside the painful and infuriating topic of Aidan, Sloan introduced herself to Pete's mother. "Your son was a fine man, Mrs. Willis. I'm so sorry for your loss."

"Thank you, dear." Her voice cracked. "It's hard knowing he was so far away from us, and we couldn't protect him."

"We're all devastated, too," Sloan said gently. "We'll bring his killer to justice. I know that doesn't help, but we want you to know we care about making things as right as we can."

"It *is* a comfort, dear. The headmistress of the Catholic school, Sister Mary Katherine, has already called a couple of times to offer her support and counseling."

"I'm glad she's able to help. I won't keep you. I just wanted to let you know we were thinking about you and your family."

"You're very kind."

"Well, good—"

"Ah, Ms. Caldwell? Before you go, I was wondering if you could pass along a message to the Sister?"

"Sure."

"I appreciate her sending out the box of Pete's things, but I was wondering if she could look again for Pete's shell neck-lace. He wore it constantly—it was one of the first beautiful things he ever made—and I was hoping to have it."

It had probably been on his body, but Sloan had no inten-tion of mentioning that possibility to his mother. She vaguely recalled seeing Pete wearing a white shell necklace made of rope. She'd check with her father. "I certainly will. Take care, Mrs. Willis."

The next phone call was to the sheriff's office. Even though it was nearly seven o'clock on a Monday night, her dad would still be working. Especially with Pete's open case looming over the island.

"Hey, Daddy," she said when he answered.

"Hey, pumpkin. Everything all right?"

Definitely not. But since she hadn't done much lately besides hole up in her condo with boxes of tissues and angry rants about how she'd shoot, skewer then barbecue Aidan Kendrick's heart over an open flame, she didn't think her dad really wanted a detailed update. "I haven't found any more bodies."

"Yippee," he said, sounding tired.

"Any new developments?"

"Nothing." And his frustration was clear. "I checked out Pete's financials, which seem to be in order. He paid his bills and ran a good little business. I talked to the Hensons and several of Pete's other clients, but nobody knows nothing."

"How did Marla Henson seem to you?"

"Cool. Collected. Definitely not the homicidal, knife-wielding type."

That had been her impression, as well.

"I can't let this go, Sloan," her dad continued.

"I know. We won't," she said fiercely. She needed something to pull her out of her anger and depression over Aidan, and this was it. "We'll all help. I think it's probably time to form an official task force."

"Already done. It'll be in the paper in the mornin'."

"Am I on it?"

"Of course. Plus my deputies, the mayor, Doc Sheppard and Hank, the bartender at Mabel's. He knows everybody and everything they do."

"Good choice. And unofficially you've got all the committee's help, plus Betsy and Patsy at the church."

Her dad sighed. "I know, honey, but don't let that get around. I can't have everybody speculatin' that I'm solving cases with kids, nuns and the Casserole Twins."

"Your secret is safe with me." At the word *secret,* she winced, her mind immediately going back to Aidan. So maybe some of the fault about the brochure was hers. Maybe she *should* have mentioned it.

But he acted as if she'd had his baby in secret, then spent twenty years lying about where it came from. It was a stupid brochure. And instead of trusting her, or even asking her nicely, he'd assumed the worst and started accusing.

"I gotta get back to it," her dad said, breaking into her thoughts. "Was that all you needed?"

"Actually, no. I just spoke with Pete's mother, and she asked about his shell necklace. She'd like to have it sent to her. Since it wasn't in the apartment, I figured it had to be on his body."

There was a long pause. "What necklace?"

"The one Pete wore. I vaguely remember it, and maybe it's generous to call it a necklace. It was more a string of shells, rope and—"

"The only thing Pete had on him were his keys. They were in his front jeans pocket. His wallet was in his truck, along with a bunch of equipment and a bag with a change of clothes. No necklace made of shells, rope or anything else."

Sloan's fingers tingled. "Are you sure?"

"I searched the clothes on his body and the truck myself."

Shaking her head, Sloan dismissed the odd sensation that she'd discovered something important. "It's probably at the apartment. Sister MK gathered his stuff. She probably didn't think it was worth anything." Though she didn't believe that for a second. "I'll go by and double-check."

"The keys are here at my office," her dad said. "Let me know what you find."

"Will do, Sheriff."

"Sheriff?"

"Since we're now working together in an official capacity, I thought I should address you in a professional manner."

"Whatever you say, pumpkin."

"And don't call me pumpkin!"

"Fine. You don't call the Catholic school headmistress, the most respected woman on the island, the woman who helped raise you, *Sister MK* to her face, do you?"

Sloan rolled her eyes. "No, Daddy. Now go home and get some rest."

Signing off, she sank onto the deck's lounge chair and watched the storm roll in. The sky turned blue, green and purple, almost all at once. The clouds met the sea and then opened up with an angry deluge of furious tears.

"You'll feel better after you cry," she whispered into the wind and leaned back into the chair cushions to watch nature's blast of emotion.

The task force would make her get over him. She'd help solve Pete's murder and eventually wouldn't care less whether the palmetto trees, brambles and bushes overtook Batherton Mansion and its owner or not. She wouldn't worry about whether he was eating or brooding or lying unconscious under the table.

Self-absorption wasn't healthy, and she wasn't much for wallowing. She'd be fine.

Though she'd rather not see or talk to Davis for a while. His prediction that Aidan would break her heart was a little too close for comfort at the moment.

Maybe he'd already gotten bored with the island and scooted back to Atlanta.

With the thunder rumbling and lightning flashing, it took her a few seconds to realize somebody was ringing her front bell, then pounding on her door. Probably somebody from the committee. Or one of her friends, concerned that they hadn't seen or heard from her in days.

She slid off the lounge chair, then headed toward the door. Dressed as she was in a faded, ratty T-shirt and fleece gym shorts, she only hoped it wasn't the venerable sister.

A giant, dripping-wet basket of flowers with worn blue jeans for legs stood in front of her.

"May I come in?" Aidan asked.

Her anger returned in a heartbeat. "Why?"

"It's our two-week anniversary."

He was completely crazy. She'd spent the last two days

cursing that she'd ever *met* him, and he thought showing up
with some lame flowers would make up for his accusations
and disgusting innuendos? She started to close the door.

"I haven't slept in two days," he said.

She paused.

"And I miss you."

Weak-kneed, she stepped aside and widened the gap in the
doorway. When he didn't move, she figured out he couldn't
see her any more than she could see him. "Put those down
before you trip over something," she said sharply.

He immediately set the arrangement down, and she noted
that he was dripping wet, as well.

"Leave them there to drain," she added, trying desperately
to ignore the exhaustion in his eyes. "You can come in if you
don't stay long."

He hesitated. "I'll drip on your carpet."

"Then *don't* come in."

She left the door open and stormed through the living area
and kitchen to the back deck. The aggravating man could
jump in the ocean for all she cared.

"It took some maneuvering to find you," he said from
behind her moments later.

"My address is unlisted because of my dad."

"I was embarrassed I had to ask someone else for it. I
never took the time to come out here before."

"So you're here now."

"Can we talk?"

"I thought we were."

She heard him walk to her, and she caught a whiff of his
familiar sandalwood scent. She closed her eyes to block out
the memories of all the times she'd inhaled his essence as
she'd taken him into her body.

His scent, mixing with the salty ocean air, aroused her, despite the way he'd doubted and hurt her.

"I'm sorry," he said softly. "I was a jerk. I know you didn't use me for a brochure or ad campaign or whatever. I know you wouldn't hurt me, but I hurt you. I have no idea why except that I think I've been relying on you too much to get over my parents, and I'm angry that I don't seem to be capable of handling things on my own."

Tears welled up in her eyes. The man of few words was suddenly spewing them like ocean-frothed whitecaps.

"Did I mention I haven't slept in two days?" he asked, his tone laced with fatigue and desperation.

Swallowing her tears, she turned and looped her arms around his neck, burying her face against his wet T-shirt. "I should have told you."

He wrapped his arms around her waist and kissed her temple. "I should have done a whole lot more."

"It's been a crazy two weeks."

"Yeah. But wonderful." He leaned back, meeting her gaze. His dark hair was glossy from the rain. "And, for the record, I *like* all the new people in my life."

Her eyes widened. "Really?"

"Mostly, I prefer just you. But I can't help thinking that if all those people had been with me in Atlanta, brainstorming, forming a task force, figuring out how to use the publicity to our advantage and all the rest, the police might have found who killed my parents."

She cupped his wet cheek. It killed her that he blamed himself. When they found Pete's killer, she hoped he'd find some peace. "Maybe. But maybe not. I'm not sure how Betsy and Patsy and their casseroles would go over at the big-city police department."

"They couldn't have hurt."

A boom of thunder echoed from the sky.

Sloan jumped and pressed into Aidan. "I'm not sure if somebody up there is happy or upset."

"Let's not take any chances." He joined their hands and started to tug her inside.

"Let's do." She wrapped her arms around his neck. "I haven't touched you in two days."

A smile tugged his lips, even as thunder rolled in the distance. "No, you certainly haven't."

By her next breath, he'd covered her mouth with his. She clung to him—warm, rain-soaked and all hers. Even in her anger over the last two days she'd craved his touch and feared she might never have him again. Touching him now, she realized she'd mourned his loss more than she wanted to admit.

She grabbed the edges of his shirt and pulled, popping buttons that flung against the screen as fast and hard as the torrents of rain falling from the charcoal-colored sky. Lightning flashed, but she wasn't afraid this time. She wanted his skin against hers. The urge to have him, touch him…keep him pounding through her as fast and insistent as her heart knocking against her ribs.

He yanked her T-shirt over her head. Her shorts and his jeans, plus underwear and her bra quickly joined the pile on the floor. Their hands were fast and greedy, running over shoulders, stomachs, backs and chests. Her fingers tangled in his wet hair, she trailed her lips along the coarse stubble on his jaw, then sank her teeth lightly into his earlobe.

His hands cupping her breasts clenched, and she moaned. Obviously taking this as a sign of encouragement, his mouth traced a heated path down her throat as his hands slid across her nipples. The calluses on his fingers were rough, as was his touch.

The insistency of their desire demanded something that

was close to violence, but without a hint of anger. She didn't want tenderness. Need crashed over her, building like a storm on the sea.

From the pile of clothes, Aidan produced a condom, which he rolled on with brisk efficiency. He fell onto the lounge chair, pulling her with him, and she straddled him, taking him inside her body.

Groaning in delight as his hardness met her softness, she dropped her head back. He braced his hands at her waist, and he raised up so his teeth could close around her nipple.

Her heart jumped. The thunder boomed overhead.

Neither she nor Aidan were in a mood to roll leisurely toward climax. He held on and moved with her plunging hips, letting her set the pace and not seeming to mind at all that her speed was a gallop rather than a comfortable trot.

She reached her peak with an explosion of pulses, and dug her fingers into his shoulders as she crested the intense, pounding waves. Vaguely, she realized he'd come, as well, and she collapsed on his chest.

Under the scent of rain and salty sea air was the sweet fragrance of magnolia from the trees behind her building. Spring humidity and the physical tango she and Aidan had performed made sweat roll down her back.

"Thanks. I needed that."

He chuckled. "My pleasure."

Content, she sighed. Then something else occurred to her, She lifted her head. "Knowing I was furious at you and you'd been a number-one ass, you came over here with condoms in your pocket?"

"I brought flowers, too," he pointed out reasonably.

"So you did." She slid off him and held out her hand to help him up. "We need to talk."

"I figured."

After they dressed, while she got him a towel to dry off his hair, he retrieved the flowers from outside. She found a vase and set the giant bouquet of roses, carnations, lilies and several other flowers she couldn't even identify on the kitchen table.

As they settled side-by-side on the sofa, she gripped his hand. "I need to explain about the brochure."

"I don't—"

She laid her finger over his lips. "I know you don't want the attention. It's fine. We'll find some other way. I just want to explain."

"It's not necessary. I—"

"I want to explain."

He nodded.

"We only wanted a picture or two," she said. "We're trying to get new members into the historical society." Embarrassed, she cleared her throat. "We need money. The properties we maintain—all two of them—need constant attention, and our funds are dangerously low. Helen thinks we need a bunch of rich tourists, and Courtney thinks we need a corporate sponsor, but ideally we'd like people like us who're interested in preserving the past and can also afford to contribute financially.

"The brochure will be an ad to attract those people, and we wanted something new, amazing and professional to make that happen. Your house is unlike anything else we have, so we wanted to feature it. Originally, we also thought it might be nice to hold a fund-raising event at the mansion one night, maybe sell or auction off a group of private tours once a year, but after realizing how much you—"

"Okay."

"Okay what?"

"Okay, you can have pictures, hold fund-raisers, a tour

and auction. And by the way, I'm a former communications mogul—or so the media always calls me—I could have helped you. You ought to be thinking radio and TV, not just print ads."

Her heart raced, but she forced skepticism into her voice. "Uh-huh. And if I'd shown up at your door two weeks ago, asking for pictures of your house, plus communications advice, you'd have jumped at the chance."

He winced. "Okay. That's fair. I probably would have slammed the door in your face." He paused, considering. "Hold on. In this imaginary scenario, would you have been wearing that red dress?"

She scowled at him.

"No? Well, you look good in everything anyway." He grinned. "And especially nothing."

She traced her finger along his thigh. "Same goes." She looked at him directly. "Are you serious about helping, letting us use the house?"

"Sure. I'll hardly notice fifty or more people trekking through."

"That's wonderful." She tried to bank her excitement that someone of Aidan's caliber and influence was willing to help them, that their dream of having Batherton Mansion as the gem of the historical society collection might come true. "*Really* wonderful. And any advice you can give us would be even better. But why? If we really go through with this, you'll have reporters tramping through your house, not just tourists and potential historical society members. Do you really want that?"

He slid his thumb over the back of her hand. "*Want* is a strong word, I guess. But I also know I can't hide from the world." His gaze met hers. "I can't pretend I don't care, or I don't need anybody."

"I had the opposite reaction after Davis left, you know. I surrounded myself with anybody and everybody. It didn't help a whole lot, either." Her gaze flicked to his. "But you did."

"And I want to do this because it will help you and people you care about. I think I'd do just about anything for you."

She stared into those intense, sincere, amazing eyes and fell in love.

It was a blink of a thought, but she knew for absolute certainty it was true.

"And I'll be your corporate sponsor." He paused, not realizing she was only falling harder and panicking more seriously with every word out of his mouth. "The non-interfering kind who doesn't require a twenty-four-foot banner with my company logo strung across the opening of the historic sites."

She cleared her throat, then managed to point out "You don't have a company."

"I will. Penelope's working through the options. Maybe an online antique business. Maybe I could start a printing company. Consulting. Or go back to communications."

"Wouldn't that involve you moving back to Atlanta or even going to someplace like New York?"

"Maybe." He paused, obviously considering. "I don't know what I'll do. I only know I'm happy where I am."

The fact that her own happiness was caught up—again—with a man she didn't know would be around long-term, but could possibly be the love of a lifetime her parents had had, was both scary and liberating.

If Pete's death and learning the details about Aidan's parents had taught her anything, it was that life could be tragically short. She needed to enjoy every moment they had, every touch, kiss and breath.

Besides, she and Aidan had known each other such a short

ime. Maybe their intense feelings would lessen. Maybe hey'd fade altogether. Maybe she'd pass him on the way in or out of Mabel's in several months, his hand linked with some cute blonde, and she'd smile and—

She jumped to her feet. "It's a woman!"

"What's a woman?" Aidan asked. "You want a woman spokesmodel for the pictures and media ads? That's probably smart. In general, more women will be willing to actively participate in historical—"

"No, no." She waved her hands impatiently. *"Oh."* She whirled and faced him, bracing her hands on his knees and pressing her lips firmly to his. "I'm so grateful you're willing to help with the brochure, the ads—all that stuff. The committee will be thrilled."

Smiling, he smoothed her hair off her face. "But…"

"I'm talking about Pete's case. A woman killed him."

Definitely not the homicidal, knife-wielding type, her dad had said about Marla. No, not at that moment. But push a passionate, in-love woman too far…and there was no limit on how crazy she could get.

"Maybe its Marla," she added, considering that possibility. "Maybe somebody else. But over the last couple of days I've been fantisizing about skewering your heart on a pike and slow-roasting it over the fire because you hurt me and—"

"I can go get more flowers," Aidan said as he stood.

She laid her hand in the center of his chest and pushed him back onto the sofa. "No, no. I was angry. I was furious. But because I have a strong moral compass and a nonviolent personality, I only had wild, ridiculous *thoughts.* What if Pete crossed some woman who wasn't so controlled?"

Aidan tentatively raised his hand. "Am I in danger of having my heart roasted over an open flame?"

"Not at the moment, no."

"Then I'll point out that *everybody* has violent thoughts. Somebody crosses you in traffic, your neighbor's dog pees on your mailbox, your kids' baseball coach doesn't recognize your child's potential major league career. People rarely act on those impulses."

"But Pete's necklace is missing."

"Oh, well that explains everything."

"But it does. Pete wore a shell necklace. Remember?"

He squinted as if trying to bring a memory into focus. "Kind of. Rope-like thing?"

"Right. It wasn't on his body, and it's not at his apartment—though I'm going over there later to double-check. If we can't find it, then the killer took it. It wasn't worth anything. It meant something *personal* to him."

"A woman killed him," Aidan said, and he sounded as certain as she was.

Sloan nodded. "I need to go by Pete's and look for the necklace again, just to be sure."

He stood, sliding his arm around her waist. "We'll both go."

"No." She walked her fingers up his chest. "You're going to the store to get champagne and steaks. We're celebrating tonight."

"Hey, Nancy Drew, we haven't caught our killer yet."

She smiled. "Not that. We're celebrating our two-week anniversary."

"Right." He angled his head and pressed his mouth softly against hers, then he briefly deepened the kiss, until her stomach was vibrating and her pulse pounded. "We'll meet at my place in about an hour?"

That seemed like a really long time away, but she nodded.

After she changed into jeans and a nicer shirt, they said a

quick goodbye in her condo building's parking lot, discovering the rain had slowed to a steady drizzle. Then she headed off to her dad's office. He insisted on coming with her to Pete's, so on the way, she explained her theory, which her dad agreed made sense. Though he didn't plan on arresting anybody just yet.

The search of the carpenter's apartment yielded no necklace, adding strength to Sloan's ideas, but the sheriff—in his practical, lawman way—reminded her they were no closer to finding the killer than before. They'd simply cut their suspect list down to one gender. People whispered about Pete being involved with several married women, but so far all those women were denying he was anything more to them than a hired carpenter.

As she drove to Aidan's she considered the idea that they'd never solve the case, and she knew she couldn't let that happen. Aidan was rejuvenated by the idea that he could make up for his past mistakes. It seemed to do little good to encourage him to move on. He needed to *do* something.

What brought you here?

Penance.

They simply *had* to find Pete's killer.

Once they did, maybe she could figure out her feelings for Aidan. Right now, she didn't see how she could tell him she loved him. He wouldn't want to hear it. It would complicate things. They were so happy and comfortable with the way things stood, especially with the project of the historical society's ad campaign to look forward to.

But not telling him felt like lying—just like the brochure.

Then again, she needed time to understand his feelings. She couldn't imagine blurting out *I love you!* in the heat of passion, only to have him say nothing. Or, worse, to say he didn't feel the same way.

For now, *I'd do just about anything for you* would have to suffice.

As she opened Aidan's door, she called his name, but got no answer. Why he'd bothered to install the lock she'd bought him when he didn't even use it was beyond her, but she guessed he'd been distracted when he'd left earlier.

For any fights they had in the future, at least she could look forward to a grand gesture when making up.

"I was hoping you'd get here first," a female voice said.

Her heart jumped, and Sloan turned toward the parlor. Marla Henson, her hand wrapped securely around a mean-looking, nickel-plated pistol, smiled.

Then again, maybe she should have told Aidan while she'd had the chance.

13

"YOU REALLY THINK we could get TV exposure?"

In the grocery store's produce section, Aidan juggled steaks, champagne and salad ingredients as he nodded at Courtney. "I know your budget's tight, so we'll make up an audition tape for one of those fixer-upper shows. They'd probably love to record the renovation process on a house like Batherton."

Courtney's smile widened. "It's so great of you to agree to help us. I told Sloan you would."

"It took some convincing," he said vaguely. He didn't want Courtney and Helen to know he'd overheard them talking Friday night, but when he'd spotted the salon owner near him in the produce section, he'd found himself wanting to share the good news right away.

In fact, he couldn't wait to get started on the project.

"But I figured you guys would bombard me with chicken casseroles until I gave in," he added.

"You're probably right."

They talked a few more minutes about fund-raisers and the possible layout for the brochure. When they parted, Courtney agreed to tell the rest of the committee about their big plans, while Aidan would ask Sloan to call a meeting as soon as possible.

He was stopped twice more in the grocery store by people he'd met over the last few weeks. As he walked to his car, he considered how much and how quickly his life had changed.

He'd come to Palmer's Island with a giant chip on his shoulder to brood alone, and a month later he was an integral part of the community. He was helping a teen learn about big business while she taught him about computers. He was preserving the history of the town where he lived. He had friends, people who cared about him.

And he had Sloan.

Their relationship seemed to be moving forward at light speed, and he wondered if they needed to slow down. He was depending on her too much. Yet he couldn't imagine not sharing everything with her—his concerns over the way he'd handled his parents' deaths, his need to make up for the past, his passion for renovating the house, his new goals to help the historical society.

But could he trust her always to be there? Was he just another friend to add to her collection? Another puzzle to solve or problem to fix? Or was there something long-lasting, something resembling forever between them?

"Why me?" Sloan asked Marla, proud that her voice trembled only slightly—a big feat since the rest of her was terrified.

"The task force," Marla replied, her dark eyes narrowed in annoyance. "All those bungling men wouldn't understand about me and Pete, but a woman might. Especially an amateur crime solver like yourself."

Her gaze fixed on the other woman's face rather than the lethal weapon in her hand, Sloan inched backward. Maybe if she kept her talking, she could distract her and somehow get out the door. Or at least hold out until Aidan—

She closed her eyes briefly. *Aidan.* What was he walking into? Was there any prayer of both of them surviving this?

Trying desperately to push away the image of Aidan's face replacing Pete's dead one, she forced herself to speak. "How do you know about the task force?"

"I have a friend at the paper."

Great. Sloan inched back another step. "How did you find me?"

"Everybody on the island knows you've been spending your nights out here."

For the first time in her life, Sloan regretted living in such a small town.

"And stop moving," Marla said sharply. "I've got big plans for you."

"What are you going to do?"

"Shoot you, of course," she said with chilling calm. "Actually, as soon as he gets here, you and your boyfriend are going to shoot each other. Everyone will assume you were fighting over Pete. Especially when I leave this clutched in your hand."

Pete's shell necklace dangled from Marla's fingers.

"Sometimes I hate it when I'm right," Sloan muttered. "Why did you kill him?"

"You're so smart, you tell me."

"You were following him and found out you weren't the only one."

Marla's eyes glittered with rage. "I was one of a *dozen.* And he thought he could just toss me aside along with all the rest and gather up a new batch. No way a man does that to *me.* I saw him head into this driveway and decided to confront him. It wouldn't have surprised me if him and that Atlanta playboy were having orgies out here." She smiled slowly. "But it was even better to find Pete was alone."

"And you figure you can add me to your bed-hopping drama?"

"You bet."

Somehow, instead of her impending death, Sloan managed to focus on Marla's grand love triangle plan and search for holes.

Several jumped out immediately.

The woman wasn't exactly a master criminal. She was a wealthy housewife who spent her days tanning and playing tennis. "My dad will never believe I was involved with Pete. Besides, both he and I already knew the necklace was missing."

Marla pursed her lips. "I suppose you figured that out?"

Sloan nodded.

"Maybe the sheriff will be too prostrate with grief to do anything," Marla said boldly. "Or maybe he won't be sheriff at all. Three murders in just over a week? He'll get fired and—"

"Even if he does, the governor will probably appoint a special investigations unit. He *is* from Charleston. He used to come here to the beach as a kid." She resisted adding *you twit*. "The case won't go away. This will never work, Marla." She held out her hand. "Give me the gun."

She laughed. "It *will* work, and it won't matter what the sheriff or anybody else thinks. They won't be able to prove anything. The only link between me and Pete will be with you—in the morgue."

"People in town know you two had an affair."

"You mean that blabbermouth hair stylist of mine?" She shrugged, seemingly unconcerned. "She doesn't have any proof, either. It'll be her word against mine."

Marla was completely confident—and utterly crazy.

Sloan was tempted to laugh herself. Marla's big scheme would never succeed. But a lot of good that would do Sloan.

She couldn't exactly giggle with I-told-you-so glee at her own funeral.

Before she could decide if she could overpower the tennis ace, or if she should fall to her knees and beg for her life, re-gretting—yet again—that she hadn't told Aidan she loved him when she had the chance, the front door flew open.

"Aidan, Sloan, where—" Courtney ground to a halt at the sight of Sloan, Marla and the gun. "Well, I'll be damned. Sloan was right."

As Sloan groaned in fear and frustration, Marla grabbed Courtney's arm and jerked her forward so that she and Sloan stood next to each other against the wall.

"*Ow*. That hurt," Courtney said, rubbing her arm.

Marla shook back her glossy dark hair. "It looks like the love triangle just became a square."

"What's she talking about?" Courtney whispered.

Sloan shook her head. "Don't ask."

"Where's Aidan? I just saw him at the store. I probably shouldn't have come over, I mean, I saw the champagne and steaks he was buying, but he told me about him helping with the brochure and ad campaign—"

"He told you about the campaign?" Sloan asked in surprise. "Did he seem excited?"

"Oh, yeah. And I thought of a really great idea, so I rushed right—"

"Would you two shut up?" Marla gestured wildly with the gun. "Sit on the steps. Now!" she added when Sloan and Courtney simply stared at her.

They rushed across the foyer, then sat.

Holding Courtney's hand, Sloan wondered with increas-ing desperation if there was any possibility of escaping this terrifying, yet somehow ridiculous, nightmare. She then noticed that the calm determination in Marla's eyes had taken on a hint of anxiety.

Would she really shoot them all? Had she ever fired a gun before? How good was her aim? She'd been pretty efficient with Pete.

Regardless, there were nine bullets in the semi-automatic Beretta she held, so that left a lot of room to make up for errors in accuracy.

As Marla began to pace, the door swung open again.

This time, it was Helen.

With a growl of rage, Marla grabbed her arm and forced her over to the stairs with Sloan and Courtney.

"Get your hand off—" Helen began, stopping when she caught sight of the gun. "Sloan, you were—"

"We all *know* she was right," Marla said furiously. "Sit down and shut up!"

Sloan very nearly smiled. Obviously, Marla shouldn't have chosen a house that was busier than an airport for her would-be homicides.

AIDAN BIT BACK a curse as he pulled into his driveway and saw Helen and Courtney's cars parked beside Sloan's convertible.

Maybe he'd been too quick to decide he liked all the new people in his life.

They could at least call before just showing up. He was going to make sure Sloan included that point of etiquette in the next agenda of the historical society meeting.

He transferred his brown-paper grocery bag to his hip—the plastic ones were banned on the island because sea turtles tended to get tangled in them—then turned the knob on the front door.

Only it wouldn't turn.

That was weird. Despite the lock Sloan had given him, he rarely used it. If he made keys for everybody who was always popping in, the whole town would have access to the house anyway.

He juggled the bag and his keys, somehow managing to get the door open without dropping either. He'd barely crossed the threshold when the sight before him registered and terror streaked down his spine.

A dark-haired woman dressed in a pale yellow tennis dress was standing in the opening to the parlor and holding a gun to Sloan's temple.

"Come on in, Mr. Kendrick," she said coolly. "We've been waiting for you."

Aidan glanced from the woman to Helen and Courtney, sitting to their right on the stairs leading to the second floor.

"Set the bag down slowly, then move over to the stairs with the ladies."

His thoughts racing, Aidan did as she asked, though he remained standing in front of the stairs, putting himself between the gun and Helen and Courtney. Somehow, he vowed to do the same with Sloan.

"We haven't met, but—"

"You're Marla Hanson."

Marla cast a look of pure fury at Sloan. "Did you tell *everybody* about me?"

"She told enough people," Aidan said. "You'll never get away with this."

"I'm really sick of people telling me that," she growled. "I was going to start by shooting her." She tapped the pistol against Sloan's temple, causing her to wince and Aidan to tighten his jaw in barely suppressed rage. "But I think you'll be first," she said, staring at Aidan.

"Okay," he returned, fighting for calm. Marla looked on the edge to him. "But can I tell Sloan something first?"

She scoffed. "What? Like some whispered plan for overpowering me and getting the gun? Do I look that stup—"

"I love you."

"I love you."

"Really?" Sloan asked, looking as surprised as he by their simultaneous confession.

He nodded, his heart feeling lighter and freer than it had in a long time. Maybe ever. "I know it's only been two weeks. I wasn't going to rush you."

"Me, either." Her eyes filled with tears. "But under the circumstances…"

He wished he could touch her. "Yeah."

"This is really sweet," Marla said in a bored tone, "but I'm ready to kill all of you now."

"*All* of us?" Helen said.

"Don't you just want to run off to Mexico?" Courtney asked. "Or maybe someplace with no extradition to the U.S., like Colombia."

Marla glared at Courtney. "You want to move to the top of the list of victims?"

Courtney pressed her lips together and shook her head.

"She makes a good point," Aidan said, not knowing what else to do except keep Marla talking as long as possible. Maybe the sheriff would show up, too. "What will killing us accomplish?"

"Yeah," Helen added. "It's not like they can lethally inject you five times."

"She could choose the chair, you know," Courtney said. "Condemned people have that option in South—"

"Shut up before I put you all in a line and just start firing!"

Marla let go of Sloan's arm and rubbed her forehead. "Let me think!"

Her other hand, the one holding the gun, had relaxed a bit, so that it wasn't pressed into Sloan's skin, but it was still resting on the side of her head. Way too close for Aidan to make an attempt to grab it.

"Okay," Marla said. "Here's how it's going to be. Nancy Drew here goes first, because you—" she gestured with the gun toward Aidan "—shot her. Then those two on the stairs go next because they walked in on you during the shooting. Then you kill yourself because you can't live with what you've done."

She smiled, not seeming to notice everyone else had gone pale. "The people on the island will believe it because you're an outsider. How long have you been here? A few weeks, isn't that right? You'll get blamed, and I'll go on to the state tennis finals."

"But he's not an outsider," Sloan said, her voice rough with emotion. "He's already one of us."

"Absolutely," Courtney said with a lift of her chin. "Ask anybody."

"That's a pretty big hole in your plan," Helen said. "I'd never believe Aidan would hurt Sloan for any reason."

"Or us, either," Courtney said boldly.

Before Aidan could feel more than a second of happiness that he'd been so easily accepted and trusted by his fellow islanders, Marla thrust Sloan at him. Instinctively, he caught her in his arms, wildly grateful to be touching her. As he looked down into her eyes, he saw all the love burning inside him reflected there. And for one wild moment, he forgot all about Marla and the imminent threat hanging over them.

"It's a good plan," Marla said suddenly, her voice dark with menace and resolve.

Aidan's gaze jumped to Marla and the gun pointed at Sloan's back.

How many times had he longed for a second chance? To go back in time and save his parents? To atone for his mistakes and make things right again?

Pleased he was getting his wish, he thrust Sloan behind him and took the bullet himself.

As IF in slow motion, Sloan watched Aidan crumple to the wooden floor and a red stain begin to spread across his shoulder.

"No!"

With a cry of rage, she rushed Marla.

Already off balance from the recoil of the gun, Marla fell backward on her butt, the pistol sailing out of her hand.

Courtney and Helen raced toward her. Courtney sat on her legs and Helen wrenched her arms behind her back. Sloan scooped up the gun, then dropped to her knees beside Aidan.

Her heart pounded as she ripped his T-shirt wide enough to check his wound.

An ugly trail was evident where the bullet had grazed his shoulder. It was bleeding heavily and probably hurt like hell, but it didn't appear life-threatening.

"She *did* have lousy aim," she said, annoyed. "I wish I'd known that twenty damn minutes ago."

"I'm going to live?" he asked, his eyes flickering open.

"Fortunately for her." She stripped off her shirt and used it to stem the flow of blood.

He winced. "Do I get any whiskey?"

"No. You get EMTs and the best painkillers the hospital can provide." She glanced over her shoulder at Courtney and Helen, who'd subdued Marla with relative ease. Maybe the historical society could branch out and sponsor self-defense classes or a neighborhood watch program. "Can one of you grab my cell phone from my purse? We need to call the sheriff and an ambulance."

"Not fortunately for you?" Aidan asked, bringing her attention back to him.

Cradling his head in her lap, she brushed his silky hair off his forehead. "What?"

"You said it was fortunate for *her* that I was alive. Not fortunately for *you?*"

Smiling, she bent forward and kissed him. "Especially for me." The adrenaline and anxiety was dissipating, replaced by a crazy high of love. Maybe she'd thank Marla one day for pushing both her and Aidan to let go of their fears and confess their feelings.

Nah. She wouldn't go that far.

"Sheriff's coming!" Courtney called out. "He said he's only a block away. He was on his way here already."

"Naturally," Aidan said with both relief and sarcasm.

Tears filled Sloan's eyes. With the danger past, the magnitude of what they'd been through was washing over her. They could have died. All of them.

And for the first time, she truly understood the depth of Aidan's loss. The confusion, the helplessness, the overwhelming fear and certainty that you hadn't done more to protect the ones you loved. "You took a bullet for me," she said in a choked voice.

His gaze met hers. The sharp, wolfish quality was still there in the silvery depths of his eyes, but now she saw an added warmth.

"I love you. I'd do anything for you."

She gave him a watery smile. "Earlier you said just about anything."

"I think we can officially eliminate that limitation."

Laughing, while keeping one hand on his wound, she cupped his cheek in her palm. "I love you."

"Love you, too."

"So, if it's all the same to you, I'd like to give up my life of fighting crime."

"Right. That'll last five minutes. What happens if somebody breaks into the church and steals Sister Mary Katherine's rosaries? Or somebody stiffs Courtney for her tip? Or even if that idiot Davis gets drunk and falls down? You'll ride to the rescue like always."

"You think?"

"I know."

"Do you mind?"

"As long as I don't have to get shot every time, no." He winced.

"Oh, my gosh, honey, let me help you."

"See what I mean? A born nurturer." His eyes glinted with satisfaction. "I'm not in too much pain, by the way. I flinched because our champagne and steak dinner is spoiling in that bag across the room. Here I was looking forward to celebrating our two-week anniversary and accepting your gratitude for my help on the historical society brochure." He grinned, his gaze dipping to the lacy pink bra she was wearing. "Complete with sexy lingerie."

"Your blood is staining the floor of your own home after escaping a homicidal tennis ace, adulterer and murderer. My shirt is currently keeping more of your life force from draining from your body. And you're thinking about sex?"

"Is that wrong?"

She grinned. "I don't think so. I like the idea of you being prone and helpless beneath me." In fact, the prospect of nursing him back to health was stimulating. Though where would she find a skimpy nurse's uniform on such short notice?

Sirens wailed in the distance.

"That'll be Daddy and the rest of the cavalry," she said, stroking his forehead. "Are you sure you're okay?"

"As long as you're not going anywhere."

"I'm sticking right here." And knowing everything was about to get crazy, and she might not have the opportunity to really tell him how she felt in that instant, she didn't hold back. "No matter how full my life has been, now it's complete. I can't imagine a day without you."

He stroked her cheek. "I feel like I've come home, like I finally belong. I don't ever want to lose you."

"You'll always have me." She bent down again and kissed him as chaos erupted around them. "And everybody else who comes along with me."

"Sloan!"

She glanced toward the door, where her gun-toting dad, a couple of deputies, Doc Sheppard and EMTs pushing a stretcher were currently bearing down on her and Aidan. She watched her dad's gaze take in Aidan lying on the floor, her bloody shirt pressed to his shoulder.

"Again?" he asked incredulously.

"Can we get a Do Not Disturb sign for the front door?" Aidan asked.

Epilogue

Three months later—June
Batherton Mansion, Palmer's Island, South Carolina

As the Pete Willis Memorial History Preservation Tour contributors and organizers filed through his house, Aidan Kendrick leaned against the opening between the parlor and the foyer and smiled.

Working with the historical society over the last few months, he, Sloan and the committee members had gone nonstop to establish a membership and marketing plan. Even Davis had provided his input, though Sloan had been careful to keep Aidan and her ex on separate tasks to avoid too many conflicts.

A nationally respected lifestyle show had documented the renovations to the house. Consequently, attention had been brought to the historical significance of the property and the island's efforts to increase its profile in the area, as well as attracting new members and capital to the society.

During the many interviews, a few reporters had connected him with the tragedies involving his parents and Pete, but with Sloan by his side, he'd managed to joke about his notoriety or divert the focus back to what was important—preserving history and the large reward for any information regarding the murder of his parents.

As if his thoughts had conjured him, John Henson walked

by, surrounded by a group of interested-in-his-every-word women.

His soon to be ex-wife's trial was due to start in a few weeks, but he was holding up pretty well. Courtney and Helen had already steered him into Sister Mary Katherine's counseling program and had hopes of fixing him up with any number of ladies.

As for Aidan, with everyone's help and encouragement, he'd established a marketing and printing business focusing on strategies and services for small, nonprofit groups. He was running the business out of the once-abandoned, but now refurbished guest cottage at the back of his property. Having graduated just two weeks earlier, Penelope had declared her independence from school and moved onto the floor above the presses.

The sheriff was openly dating Mabel, the diner queen. Which Sloan pretended only to tolerate, even though Aidan knew she was thrilled her father had caught the romance bug.

As Sloan passed by him, no doubt on her way to the kitchen to see if she could help Betsy and Patsy with the catering efforts, he snagged her wrist and pulled her against him. "Let's elope."

"We already have a wedding date. The second Saturday in September."

He dipped his head, nuzzling her neck to inhale her familiar tropical scent. "Too far away."

"What will you get then that you don't have now?"

Linking her left hand with his, the band of her engagement ring brushing his fingers, he tried to remember the TV cameramen, their friends, the paid guests and supporters of the society, plus her father moving around. "You, forever."

"You already have that."

"I want it officially. I still think Davis harbors reunion fantasies."

Sloan shrugged. "Please. Every time he runs off to Atlanta for another job interview, he brings back a different woman."

Aidan sighed. "It's so transparent. He's trying way too hard to fill my playboy shoes."

"*Former* playboy," his future bride said, her gaze fusing with his.

"Former," he agreed. "You're all I'll ever need."

Love, as always, shone from her eyes as she looked at him. "Me, too."

Seeming to not care how many folks surrounded them, she snuggled close and rested her head against his shoulder. "How soon do you think we can get rid of all these people?"

"You—get rid of people?" He felt her forehead. "Are you sure you aren't sick?"

Pushing back, she swatted his shoulder. "Fine, then, I'll just go back to work." Her eyes twinkled. "Somebody has to count all the money we've made tonight."

"Excuse me."

Aidan turned to see a man of small-stature, with a gray mustache and beard, standing beside him. "Aren't you the owner of this property?"

"Yes, sir, I am." He held out his hand. "Aidan Kendrick."

"Charles Sweeney," the other man said. "My wife and I having been vacationing on the island for years now, and we never knew this house was here. We joined the society just last week."

Aidan smiled. "We're so glad to have you."

"It's important work, preserving the past. But I wonder if you wouldn't mind answering a brief question, Mr. Kendrick?"

Used by now to the curiosity of tourists and reporters alike, Aidan nodded. "Anything."

"What's that?"

Turning his head, Aidan realized the new society member was pointing at the spot beside the stairs where the bullet that that grazed him months ago had lodged.

Though the sheriff had taken the slug into evidence, Aidan had left the scar in the wall, curiously similar to the one on his shoulder, to remind himself of what was important. That giving yourself completely to the ones you loved mattered above all else. To live every day as if it was your last.

Yesterday was over, but you could learn from your mistakes and become the person you truly want, and deserve, to be.

He wanted to explain all that, but wasn't entirely sure how to start when he remembered Helen telling him just that morning, *Don't forget...people love a juicy story.*

With a perfectly straight face, he nodded importantly. "That, sir, is the spot where Henrietta Masters Palmerton was shot as she fought off a whole regiment of Union soldiers while defending her wounded husband and her house from invaders."

Sloan, standing next to him, frowned.

He simply winked at her. They'd all been through enough tragedy. He figured they deserved some humor.

Mr. Sweeney was amazed. "Why, that's remarkable."

"It's also completely made up," Aidan admitted. "Actually, sir, that mark represents the moment my life nearly ended and actually began."

Mr. Sweeney's eyes grew wider. "Does it now?"

Aidan laid his hand on the other man's shoulder. "You like whiskey? How about I get us some glasses and tell you all about it?"

Before he led his new friend toward the bar, Aidan glanced back at Sloan.

Yeah, his life was just beginning.

* * * * *

Celebrate 60 years of pure reading pleasure
with Harlequin® Books!

Harlequin Romance® is celebrating by showering you
with DIAMOND BRIDES *in February 2009.*
Six stories that promise to bring a touch of sparkle
to your life, with diamond proposals
and dazzling weddings, sparkling brides
and gorgeous grooms!

Enjoy a sneak peek at Caroline Anderson's
TWO LITTLE MIRACLES,
available February 2009
from Harlequin Romance®.

'I'VE FOUND HER.'

Max froze.

It was what he'd been waiting for since June, but now—now he was almost afraid to voice the question. His heart stalling, he leaned slowly back in his chair and scoured the investigator's face for clues. 'Where?' he asked, and his voice sounded rough and unused, like a rusty hinge.

'In Suffolk. She's living in a cottage.'

Living. His heart crashed back to life, and he sucked in a long, slow breath. All these months he'd feared—

'Is she well?'

'Yes, she's well.'

He had to force himself to ask the next question. 'Alone?'

The man paused. 'No. The cottage belongs to a man called John Blake. He's working away at the moment, but he comes and goes.'

God. He felt sick. So sick he hardly registered the next few words, but then gradually they sank in. 'She's got *what?*'

'Babies. Twin girls. They're eight months old.'

'Eight—?' he echoed under his breath. 'They must be his.'

He was thinking out loud, but the P.I. heard and corrected him.

'Apparently not. I gather they're hers. She's been there since mid-January last year, and they were born during the summer—June, the woman in the post office thought. She was more than helpful. I think there's been a certain amount of speculation about their relationship.'

He'd just bet there had. God, he was going to kill her. Or Blake. Maybe both of them.

'Of course, looking at the dates, she was presumably pregnant when she left you, so they could be yours, or she could have been having an affair with this Blake character before…'

He glared at the unfortunate P.I. 'Just stick to your job. I can do the math,' he snapped, swallowing the unpalatable possibility that she'd been unfaithful to him before she'd left. 'Where is she? I want the address.'

'It's all in here,' the man said, sliding a large envelope across the desk to him. 'With my invoice.'

'I'll get it seen to. Thank you.'

'If there's anything else you need, Mr Gallagher, any further information—'

'I'll be in touch.'

'The woman in the post office told me Blake was away at the moment, if that helps,' he added quietly, and opened the door.

Max stared down at the envelope, hardly daring to open it, but when the door clicked softly shut behind the P.I., he eased up the flap, tipped it and felt his breath jam in his throat as the photos spilled out over the desk.

Oh, Lord, she looked gorgeous. Different, though. It took him a moment to recognise her, because she'd grown her hair, and it was tied back in a ponytail, making her look younger and somehow freer. The blond highlights were gone, and it was back to its natural soft golden-brown, with a little curl in the end of the ponytail that he wanted to thread his finger through and tug, just gently, to draw her back to him.

Crazy. She'd put on a little weight, but it suited her. She looked well and happy and beautiful, but oddly, considering how desperate he'd been for news of her for the past year— one year, three weeks and two days, to be exact—it wasn't only Julia who held his attention after the initial shock. It was the babies sitting side by side in a supermarket trolley. Two identical and absolutely beautiful little girls.

* * * * *

When Max Gallagher hires a P.I. to find his estranged wife, Julia, he discovers she's not alone—she has twin baby girls, and they might be his. Now workaholic Max has just two weeks to prove that he can be a wonderful husband and father to the family he wants to treasure.

Look for TWO LITTLE MIRACLES
by Caroline Anderson,
available February 2009
from Harlequin Romance®.

HARLEQUIN® *Romance*®

This February the Harlequin® Romance series will feature six Diamond Brides stories featuring diamond proposals and gorgeous grooms.

Share your dream wedding proposal and you could WIN!

The most romantic entry will win a diamond necklace and will inspire a proposal in one of our upcoming Diamond Grooms books in 2010.

In 100 words or less, tell us the most romantic way that you dream of being proposed to.

For more information, and to enter the Diamond Brides Proposal contest, please visit **www.DiamondBridesProposal.com**

Or mail your entry to us at:
IN THE U.S.: 3010 Walden Ave., P.O. Box 9069, Buffalo, NY 14269-9069
IN CANADA: 225 Duncan Mill Road, Don Mills, ON M3B 3K9

REQUEST YOUR FREE BOOKS!

2 FREE NOVELS PLUS 2 FREE GIFTS!

HARLEQUIN®

Blaze™

Red-hot reads!

YES! Please send me 2 FREE Harlequin® Blaze™ novels and my 2 FREE gifts (gifts are worth about $10). After receiving them, if I don't wish to receive any more books, I can return the shipping statement marked "cancel." If I don't cancel, I will receive 6 brand-new novels every month and be billed just $4.24 per book in the U.S. or $4.71 per book in Canada, plus 25¢ shipping and handling per book and applicable taxes, if any*. That's a savings of 15% or more off the cover price! I understand that accepting the 2 free books and gifts places me under no obligation to buy anything. I can always return a shipment and cancel at any time. Even if I never buy another book, the two free books and gifts are mine to keep forever.

151 HDN ERVA 351 HDN ERUX

Name   (PLEASE PRINT)

Address   Apt. #

City   State/Prov.   Zip/Postal Code

Signature (if under 18, a parent or guardian must sign)

Mail to the **Harlequin Reader Service:**
IN U.S.A.: P.O. Box 1867, Buffalo, NY 14240-1867
IN CANADA: P.O. Box 609, Fort Erie, Ontario L2A 5X3

Not valid to current subscribers of Harlequin Blaze books.

Want to try two free books from another line?
Call 1-800-873-8635 or visit www.morefreebooks.com.

* Terms and prices subject to change without notice. N.Y. residents add applicable sales tax. Canadian residents will be charged applicable provincial taxes and GST. Offer not valid in Quebec. This offer is limited to one order per household. All orders subject to approval. Credit or debit balances in a customer's account(s) may be offset by any other outstanding balance owed by or to the customer. Please allow 4 to 6 weeks for delivery. Offer available while quantities last.

Your Privacy: Harlequin Books is committed to protecting your privacy. Our Privacy Policy is available online at www.eHarlequin.com or upon request from the Reader Service. From time to time we make our lists of customers available to reputable third parties who may have a product or service of interest to you. If you would prefer we not share your name and address, please check here. ☐

HB08R

HARLEQUIN *Blaze*™

COMING NEXT MONTH

#447 BLAZING BEDTIME STORIES Kimberly Raye, Leslie Kelly, Rhonda Nelson
Who said fairy tales are just for kids? Three intrepid Blaze heroines decide to take a break from reality—and discover, to their personal satisfaction, just how sexy happily-ever-afters can be....

#448 SOMETHING WICKED Julie Leto
Josie Vargas has always believed in love at first sight—and once she meets lawman Rick Fernandez, she's a goner. If only he didn't have those demons stalking her....

#449 THE CONCUBINE Jade Lee
Blaze Historicals
Chen Ji Yue has the chance to bring the ultimate honor to her family if she is chosen as one of the new emperor's wives. Of course, first she has to beat out the other three hundred virgins vying for the position. And then she has to stay out of the bed of Sun Bo Tao, the emperor's best friend.

#450 SHE THINKS HER EX IS SEXY... Joanne Rock
24 Hours: Lost
After a very public quarrel with her boyfriend, rock star Romeo Jinks, actress Shannon Leigh just wants to get her life back. But when she finds herself stranded in the Sonoran Desert with her ex, she learns that great sex can make breaking up hard to do.

#451 ABLE-BODIED Karen Foley
Uniformly Hot!
Delta Force operator Ransom Bennett is used to handling anything that comes his way. But debilitating headaches have put him almost out of action. Luckily, his new neighbor, Hannah Hartwell, knows how to handle his pain...and him, too.

#452 UNDER THE INFLUENCE Nancy Warren
Forbidden Fantasies
Sexy bartender Johnny Santini mixes one wicked martini. Or so business exec Natalie Fanshaw discovers, sitting at his bar one lonely Valentine's night. Could a fling with him be a recipe for disaster? Well, she could always claim to be under the influence....

www.eHarlequin.com

HBCNMBPA0109R2